Reflections

of a

ROLLING STONE

SANDY WILLS

Editor: Adrienne Michelle Horn

Printed in the United States of America.

ISBN 978-1-7346495-0-5

I would like to dedicate this book to my father and mother, Ike and Jere Williams. I am grateful for your unwavering love and support, and I feel so blessed to have you as my parents.

Cousin Luverinda,
Best Wishes

— Ki

PROLOGUE

Look at them! All decked out in their Sunday best to come and say wonderful things about me, I guess. Humph. I wonder how long this homegoing service is going to last. One thing I can say for sure -- looking over this crowd at my family -- I did a damn good job. My legacy is strong, and I know that they will get along fine without me. Hell, I raised them all, so some of me must have rubbed off on them. That could only make them better because I, Kendall Sanford, was the best damn thing to come out of McIntosh County, Georgia.

You are probably wondering why I am visiting my own funeral, right? Well, I haven't been called up for judgment yet, so I wanted to take a peek at what my kids have been up to since I left this earthly place. I am glad they followed my wishes and had me cremated. I did not want people gawking at me. Most of these folks would not have so much as spit on me last week when I was living. Now they are paying final respects when they could have stayed home and watched the Bulldogs whoop up on them Gators. People are funny that way. They will spend hundreds of dollars on flowers for your funeral when you die but not give you a penny while you living. Yeah, I said it. And I meant it, too. Talk about hypocrisy. Well, that will lead us into a whole other story. Let me focus back on why I am here.

All six of my kids are here to honor me as their father. Uh oh. Are all of their mothers here, too? This could get a little tricky. You see, I have six kids by four different women. Though they all may not have grown up in the same house, I loved each one of my kids and did everything for them that any man could humanly do. I just want to make that perfectly clear before anyone gets the wrong idea about the type of man or father I am. Well… was.

Let's see. In birth order, I have my oldest son, Kendall Jr., Kenneth by Donna, the twins, Kimberly and Kenleigh, by the love of my life, Ava Lynn, Lamont by Kathi, and the baby, Karissa Joy. All of my kid's names started with "K" -- well almost all. That way there was no question about whose they were. I claimed all of my kids. I knew who I had slept with, and when I slept with them, so it was no need to pretend as if I was not their daddy.

My oldest and my youngest were from my wife, Cynthia. We were married for sixty years, and not once did this woman leave my side. I will be honest…I probably would have left me a long time ago. When that preacher said, "'til death do you part," she won that race. So now she is free of me and can enjoy this time as a single woman. I hope that the next man will treat her better than I did, but everyone knows that whoever he is won't be able to make her feel as good as I made her feel.

That is one thing about myself that I am willing to bet good money on. I knew how to make love to a woman real good. Once we were together, they just couldn't get enough of me. I had Cynt whipped. It was the only logical explanation as to why she stayed with me all these years. As you should've figured out by now, I had four outside children on her, but on top of all of that, I had some other addictions, too.

My life was interesting, to say the least. Now I am here, and it is all said and done. There is an old gospel song that says, "When I look back over my life, and I think things over, I can truly say that I've been blessed. I have a testimony." My testimony is simply my life story, or better yet, a reflection on how I remember things as they happened over the seventy-eight years I spent on earth. Here is my testimony…

Chapter 1

The sound of an old diesel pulpwood truck pulling into the truck yard roared over the *Lone Ranger* theme song, which indicated the show was starting to play on the small Zenith that Pops had in his office. We kids, well the boys anyway, would watch it whenever we were at work with him. He made us work hard because he believed a man had to earn his keep. However, in between loading logs or helping with maintenance on his fleet of trucks, he did allow us to be kids. We could watch our favorite programs of that time, such as *Howdy Doody* and The Ed Sullivan Show. I remember my favorite show of all being the Lone Ranger at ten years old in 1950. He was so cool, and the fight scenes were exciting to a young ruckus country boy like me.

My Pops was a businessman, one of the few black business owners in our area at the time. He owned a trucking company that ran pulpwood for the local paper mills. This was a dirty job, but you could make an honest living with nice pay for it back then.

The office was located in Darien, which sits between the two cities with the biggest paper mills in Georgia -- Savannah and Brunswick. We had trucks running to both mills all week long. My dad always kept a strong crew of loaders and drivers, which meant he had money coming in. He kept clothes on our backs and food on the table.

For niggers… Oh, wait. Excuse me. I mean, for NEGROES, it wasn't normal to see this sort of thing where we came from. Actually, it was uncommon to see it during that time anywhere. But it was definitely uncommon in Southeast Georgia. My Pops had one advantage, though.

Most of the time, people who first saw him never knew if he was white, black, or Indian. Folks just flat out couldn't tell and didn't know what to make of him. Once they found out he was colored, they were already making money, so they really didn't care.

Boy, I remember one story Pops told us about when he was riding the bus in Savannah. He said he boarded the bus, paid his fair like everyone else, and immediately sat behind the driver. The bus ride went along just fine. Standing on the corner as he was getting off the bus was Ole Yella. He grabbed my Pops and gave him one of those big hugs older men give when they greet one another. "Mannnnnnnnn! Look at you, Partna. I ain't seen you in about a month of Sundays." All of my Pops friends called him Partna. People in the Deep South are known for having nicknames that have nothing to do with their real names.

"Yella!" my Pops screamed back as he was walking down the steps to get off the bus. Wouldn't you know it, that bus driver caught on real quick that he had let a colored man sit in the whites-only section of his bus. My Pops said that white man turned about fifteen different shades of red as he glared at him.

"Look here, boy. Don't think I haven't figured out what you just did. It's miscegenated niggers like you that make it hard for us trying to follow the law around here. I better not catch you on another bus in this city, boy, or I'll get some good old boys to come have a talk with you."

Pops just tipped his hat at that bus driver, smiled inside, and kept on talking to Ole Yella. My Pops said in this world you have to choose your battles wisely, and that particular day, he felt he had already won because he had gotten where he was going. Pops was funny in that way. He never got too flustered and seemed to make his way in this world that was not particularly kind to folks like us. That was Pops. He was as cool as a cucumber.

With Pops being a businessman, the women in town always seemed extra nice to him. What I was told as I got older was that Sanford men all had a way with women. Thinking back on it now, women would always smile and tend to Pops extra special. I remember the way that Mrs. Bessy would always ask, "How do, Mr. Sanford?" all breathy and drawn out as she leaned over the counter at the general store. "Anythang I can get you and these chillun ta'day, baby?" Pops would just tip his hat and smile.

Mrs. Bessy sure could make a young boy feel all warm inside even if her aim was at Pops. She always had on something extra tight that made her titties look bigger than what they already were. I mean they were huge, and you could not help but stare. They were always propped up real high and made your mind wander off to what it would be like to hold them in your hands. When Mama would ask me to walk down to the general store for something that she might have needed, there was never any argument from me. That's because I hoped that Mrs. Bessy would be there instead of her husband.

Mr. Bessy was a mean ol' man that no one in Darien liked too much. Most folks said the only reason that Mrs. Bessy was married was for the money that she thought she would get once he died. She was about twenty years younger than he was and his second wife. How somebody that ugly and mean got someone that looked like her, I will never understand. There must be some truth to that old saying, "Money can make any man look good in a woman's eyes." After the first Mrs. Bessy went on to be with the Lord, he took up with the new Mrs. Bessy shortly after that, and now getting a treat at the store has a completely new meaning for me.

"Nathaniel!" I could hear Mama screaming for Pops from the back door of the house. He was out working in the field near Mama's greens. It was a Saturday evening in late July 'round about dusk. The summertime in southeast Georgia is best known for a couple of things. The sweltering heat is accompanied by humidity so thick you feel like you can cut it with a knife. Then there are what I think to be the creatures created by the devil himself -- sand gnats. If you ever have the pleasure of walking into a swarm of gnats, it feels like they take over your body and immediately turn you into a flailing idiot. Things can be going just fine, and then BAM! You feel things flying into your nose, mouth, and ears all at the same time. You have not had a complete childhood experience in the South if you have not swallowed at least a million of these while riding your bike. Somehow, they can find their way into every hole in your head and wreak havoc. It is a sight to see someone choking, swatting, and blowing air out of their nose at the same time trying to get rid of the little critters.

I looked out into the field where Pops was and saw him look up after Mama called his name. He bellowed out, "Be there directly, Sug!" When Southerners tell you they are going to do something directly, that means they are about to do it soon. I saw him put down the bag that he was piling greens into, and he began to take long strides towards the house. You could tell by the way that he walked that he was a take-charge kind of person. I always tried to emulate that walk, but my brothers always gave me a hard time, usually accompanied by a few fist lumps for making them look bad.

I hustled around to the front of the house to play near the porch where Mama was standing so I could eavesdrop and hear what she had to tell him. She would only call him out of the field for something important. That is why I knew whatever she had to tell him it must have been juicy.

"Nathaniel, you got this here telegram that come when the postman dropped off the mail this evening. Telegram come in from Savannah. I figured it must be pretty important." Mama held it out to him with a longing look in her eyes. She was always my Pops biggest cheerleader, and she prided herself on being the wife of a successful man. You could tell by the excitement that danced in her eyes that she knew it was some good news about his work with the paper mills in Savannah. "Open it and tell me what it say."

He took that piece of paper from Mama with the biggest smile on his face. As Pops read the telegram, you could see that something was wrong since his face turned white. Not white like as in a white person because he was already there, but white like people do when they are spooked by something.

"What is it, Nathaniel? Is everything alright?" Now Mama had that worried look on her face.

He just turned and walked back down off the porch into the field to finish picking his greens.

I thought to myself, *that did not go as any of us thought it would.* Yet, I do not think Mama or me could anticipate what was to come in the following days.

That night after the telegram incident, Pops still hadn't said a word about what he had read. He just came in from the field, washed up and headed out to the Bluff to the Red Derby. He did not even touch his dinner, and Mama made his favorite meal to eat on a Saturday night -- stewed okra and tomato soup over rice. My brothers and I knew something was really bothering him. All we could do was hope that no one was dead or that Pops was not being drafted to fight in a war.

There was a rumor floating around that Uncle Sam was calling up all men over 17 to go fight in Korea. And all meant all. No age was off-limits. I was too young at the time, but Pops and my oldest brother fit that description. I was willing to bet anything that the telegram was actually a draft letter to tell him "Your Country Needs You!" All I could imagine was an old pine box with an American flag sitting in the front of Third Street Baptist Church with Pops laying inside of it, and my Mama, brothers and I standing around crying. I needed to find out what that telegram from Savannah said, or my imagination was going to get the best of me.

Chapter 2

The Red Derby was one of the juke joints that was out in the backwoods near Darien. Grandma Mag always would tell Pops that he shouldn't go to that place and leave his wife at home with the kids. She would say, "Nate, you my son. Now let me tell you ain't nothing up there at tha' Derby but lickah and loose women. Is that what you going for, huh?! Them loose women?! You gone catch that nasty disease and die! Keep on and see what I tell ya'." Pops would hear her, but he always ignored her. That was his time away from it all – when he got to be with his friends and unwind.

The smell of the air in the Brown Derby was a mixture of cigarette smoke and brown liquor. I knew it well because anytime Pops had been there his shirts in the dirty laundry pile would have that smell in them until Mama washed his clothes. A traveling band was playing that night, and the lead singer was belting out Hoochie Coochie Mama and swaying her hips to the beat as if she was making love to the air. All of the men in the place howled as she was winding, and it made them squeeze the women they were dancing with a little tighter on their bottoms. Pops walked into that place and seemed to fit right in. The bartender gave him a glass of special hooch. He took a sip of the sweet brown liquor and observed the place until his eyes landed on where he would stay to for the rest of the night.

"What ya say, fellas? Can I get in on the next hand?"

"Hey, Partna! We didn't see you sneak in here," said Buster Tate, the owner of the club.

"What say, Busta?" Pops asked with that familiarity that longtime friends have.

"I can't call it. You just in time. He got to go home and beg his woman to take him back," Buster said, pointing to his spades partner as he laughed. The man just waved off Buster, gave Pops a handshake, and left the spot open for him to take his place at the table.

Pops stayed at that card table for hours to avoid telling his wife what was in that telegram. He went home a little before dawn and slipped into bed like nothing had happened.

Sunday afternoon, about the same time we were getting home from church, a white truck pulled up into our yard with some folks we ain't never seen before around these parts. The man that was driving was the biggest man I had ever seen in my entire ten years on this earth. His body seemed to have taken up an entire three-fourths of the pickup truck cab, which I guess it was a good thing that the woman riding with him was teeny tiny, or else she would have had to get in the bed of the truck, like us kids do in the back of Pops truck.

When the man got out of the truck, he seemed even bigger than he did stuffed inside the cab. It was like watching a jack-in-the-box pop out at the end of the song after being folded down inside for so long. He stood about six foot ten inches tall if not taller, and he had to weigh near four hundred pounds. I think he was considered a giant among us, literally.

"Hey there, ma'am. My name is Benny Lee Jackson. I come down today from Savannah, and I am looking for someone by the name Nathaniel Sanford. Is he here?" the giant asked as he approached Mama.

"Well, that is my husband, Mr. Jackson. What bidness you got with him? Let me know, and I will go and get him for you," Mama said, standing in front of us kids as if to shield us from the giant, though I am not entirely sure on what she could do seeing how big he was. Most all of us boys were taller than her already, and although she wasn't small, she wasn't hardly big either.

The giant looked down at the brick-paved pathway that was leading to our front door first. Then he looked over to the woman he came with and then back down at the ground again. "Mrs. Sanford, if you could just let him know that I got some business to go over with him that he needs to know about, I would certainly appreciate it."

I could tell Mama didn't like the sound of that response, but she motioned towards Kevin and Lester and told them to go hunt for Pops and let him know that company was here.

"Well, Mr. Jackson, since you and…" Mama hesitated at first, then finished after coming to the conclusion that they were together, "Mrs. Jackson done come all the way from Savannah, would you like a cool drink while you wait for my Nathaniel?"

"No, ma'am. We will just wait right here for Nathaniel. Once I say what I got to say I want to get back on down the road. I sent him a telegram letting him know that I would be coming today. Do you know if he got it?"

Now Mama's eyebrows went together, and her nostrils flared out. She only did that when she thought something was about to run amok or something irritated her real bad.

She started talking real slow like, "Why, yes. We did receive a telegram yesterday evening around about this same time. Nathaniel didn't tell me that we were expecting company today though," she paused. "My boys are going to find their daddy. He should be out directly." She pursed her lips together, then continued. "Excuse me for just one moment. I need to go warm up my pots for our Sunday dinner."

If I know one thing about my Mama, I know her Sunday dinner has been prepped, and everything was left on warm in the oven before we went to church. So, all of that talk was just for show so she could excuse herself. When she went into the house, I followed her so I could see where she was going. Just as I suspected, she made a beeline for the trunk that was in the corner by her room. That is where Pops kept all the hunting shotguns. She pulled out the mahogany brown one, which she would use in contests at the annual County Fair. Mama was one of the best shots in McIntosh County. I have seen her line matches up on a fence post and shoot every one of them suckers off. Most folks knew that she was handy with her gun, but I was praying that this man didn't find out firsthand just how handy she was.

Mama was moving so fast. She must have been scared of how big the giant was and mad at Pops for what he must have done to have some man come looking for him. She started to mumble under her breath, "This better not be about no woman Nay-Than-Yell or I might just let this big nigger kill you." Mama was loading the gun and moving around so fast that she forgot that I was standing there. Cuss words and guarantees were flowing out of her mouth like she was possessed. I was shocked that Mama even knew most of these words, let alone using them on the Lord's day. Up until then, the only words I heard her use on a Sunday were "Praise the Lord" and "Pass the peas." I wasn't sure if I needed to run and tell Pops not to come out. Because if this man was here to kill him for running around with his wife, Mama might just beat the giant to it.

I decided to let her alone so that I wasn't on the other end of her wrath. She rambled for another few seconds while she loaded the gun and then walked back towards the front door. Right before she went back out in the yard where our visitors still stood waiting for Pops, she set the shotgun against the doorjamb just out of sight. I figured she put it there so that it was easy to access just in case this visitor was not so friendly after all. If he meant to bring harm to anyone in this family, boy, he was going to be in for a surprise even bigger than he was.

Mama sashayed back out onto the front porch as if she had not a care in the world. She looked down on the giant and the woman still standing on the brick path and said, "I hear the boys stirring. I think they out looking for him in the back garden. It shouldn't be too long now before he comes up here." She gestured her hand to one of the trees in the front yard. "We have some seats under the shade. We can catch a cool breeze if you all would like to follow me and wait for Nathaniel over this way."

"If you don't mind ma'am, we will just wait right here," said the giant looking all strange at the woman we assumed was his wife.

Mama's nostrils flared, and her eyebrows went together again. And well, folks, that was it for southern hospitality. She was about to blow. She shifted over to one side and tilted her head just so. That was when I knew she had had about enough of these strangers.

"Looky here, Mr. Jackson, and you, too, Mrs. Jackson," she said, puffing up, "I done offered you a cool drink and a place to take a seat and rest after your road trip and you still ain't even tell me why you in my front yard a' looking for my husband. I'm beginning to get real uneasy, so I'm gon' ask you just one more time. What bidness you got wit Nay-Than-Yell?"

You could tell how upset Mama was by how she said Pops' name. She only said every syllable that hard when she was mad. Between the telegram, Pops not telling her what was on it, and these strangers at her doorstep not telling her what this was all about, she was hotter than grease at a Friday night fish fry.

Just then, the tiniest of little whimpers came from the cab of the truck. The teeny-tiny woman had left her door open. Mama and I slowly began to realize that those whimpers were actually from a baby crying. The teeny-tiny woman went to the cab of the truck and pulled out a small basket. A few moments later, she lifted a baby out and began to rock it, saying, "Everything is gonna be alright." From where I was standing, the baby looked like a little white baby. The giant cast his eyes down on the bricks one more time, and then he began to speak to Mama very slow and careful. I guess he figured he had aggravated her enough, so he had better be gentle when talking to her.

"Mrs. Sanford, I have a sister by the name of Peach Jackson. Well, I had a sister. You see she died during childbirth up in Savannah about a week ago. We had a midwife for her and all, but her body just didn't take too kindly to this here baby being born into the world."

Mama interrupted, "Well, I am so sorry to hear about your sister. Mr. Jackson, why are you here, sir?"

"Well, this here baby's name is Janie Mae. Her mother is dead, and me and my wife here cannot raise her on account of my wife being sick." That explained why she looked so frail. "So, I brung her down here so her Pa could take her." He paused, and you could tell in his eyes that he was sorry. "Ma'am, Nathaniel Sanford is this here baby's Pa."

Mama did not move. She just stood there frozen, staring at the man who just told her that her husband had had a child outside of the home that they had been building together for so many years. My mind went numb, but my eyes stayed fixed on Mama. I would have to stop her if she decided to do something crazy like shoot the man, his wife, or that little baby.

No sooner than Mr. Jackson stopped talking, my brothers came running up to the front yard with Pops right behind them. Kevin and Lester stopped right next to me, and Pops went up to the giant, shook his hand, and said, "So I think I know what you are here for." He went over and grabbed the baby from the teeny tiny woman and began looking at her. She cooed like a baby does when its Daddy is holding it. While Pops stood there rocking the baby, the couple put the basket and a bag of stuff, which I am assuming was for the baby, on the brick path. The man tipped his hat then they got in the car and drove off. All we could see was dust kicking up from their tires as they pulled off down the dirt road.

Mama, my two brothers, and I just stood in the yard staring at Pops, while he was still rocking the baby. He finally looked up at Mama and said, "Well, Sug, looks like we got us a girl, finally."

Chapter 3

Looking at Janie Mae run around the house so excited to be going to her first day of kindergarten was a spectacle that made all of us smile. Who would have thought that the day that she came into our lives happiness would have been the outcome? With everything inside of me, I just knew that story was going to end up differently.

My imagination showed me Mama reaching inside the door, grabbing the gun, and killing the only man I'd ever called Pops. I sure am glad that was strictly my imagination and that things did work out for the best. Sure, it was touch and go there for a long time with long fits of crying from Mama, yelling and screaming between my parents, and the long droughts of them not speaking to one another, but they found a way to get through it.

Mama was so worked up after one of the fights that she and Pops had that she disappeared for a whole week and we thought she was never coming back. Come to find out, she was held up over at Aunt Sandra's house over in Ludowici, which was surprising as bad as Aunt Sandra grates on Mama's nerves. I have heard her say more than once, "Me and Sandy was raised the exact same, so I don't know how she keeps such a nasty house. Roaches all up and through her house. Don't make no sense to me." I guess Mama figured dealing with Pops was better than living amongst filth and insects that like to crawl on you in your sleep.

Somehow, she managed to get past the hurt and grew to love Janie Mae. It took a while, but a few months in, if you didn't know the back story, you wouldn't know that Mama didn't give birth to that child herself. She made so many pretty dresses, showed her off to everyone, and loved on her so hard. It was as if she wanted to make up for her Mama dying and wanted to make her feel extra special because of it. She was also the apple of Pops' eye; she was the true definition of a "baby girl." Though she was spoiled rotten, she was also a very sweet little girl, which is why I took great pride in being the big brother that had the honor of walking her into her first day of kindergarten.

"Janie Mae, are you excited that you get to go to school now? What are you going to do great? I know you will be great at reading and writing because you are real smart. And you're real pretty, too. Also, you can let the little kindergarten boys know that you got three big brothers, so they bet not mess with you." This was how our conversation went as we rode the bus into town. The colored school was on one side of town, and the white schools were on the other side of the town. Since it was such a small community, elementary, middle, and high school were all under one roof.

We pulled into the driveway of Ralph Bunche School (that is the new name that our school had just gotten a few years back). When I started kindergarten, it was called the McIntosh County School for the Colored. It was changed when Ralph Bunche, a colored man, became the Nobel Peace Prize winner in 1950. It was something special that a black man had gotten that honor, and all the parents in the community rallied together to make the name change happen. They felt like with that name, their kids would know who he was and realize they could do something just as special as he had.

As a teenager that hated school, I was glad that my Pops owned a company. I looked forward to going into the family business after high school. I sure didn't want to go to anybody's war like my oldest brother, Lester. His pictures of the women over in Korea might have made you want to go, but the stories reminded you that war was not all fun and games. There was lots of death and no contact with your family. The worst cases came back to their Mamas in a pine box. Lester was lucky.

19

He was sent home after a land mine exploded and he was hit in the ass with shrapnel. Some of his army buddies were not so lucky.

After I dropped off Janie Mae to her kindergarten class with Mrs. Geraldine, who was also our church pianist, I walked over to the high school wing. It was amazing to see how people you grew up with looked so different once you got to high school. One girl in particular who had definitely changed for the better over the summer break was Ava Lynn Jefferson. She was about the prettiest thing I had laid eyes on since Mrs. Bessy.

I saw her as soon as I entered the classroom, and I wasn't the only guy paying her some attention. Ike Willie was already jawing in her ear about something, but I knew she wasn't paying him no mind because as soon as she saw me, she started smiling and those big ol' dimples popped out for the world to see. Right then, I knew she was going to be mine, and I was going to be hers. I let old Ike finish without me bothering him. When we let out for lunch, I did not even have to go up to her. We just sort of got close to each other. We ended up talking through our entire lunchtime together every day all the way up to her birthday in January. She would be turning sixteen, which meant I would be able to take her out on a date, or so I thought.

"Ava Lynn, what are you doing for your birthday this weekend," I asked her with a smirk on my face.

"Well, my Mom is baking a cake, and I can invite some of my girlfriends over Saturday for a sleepover." She continued, "Kendall Sanford, what are you going to bring me for my birthday? You know I will be sixteen now, so I will be able to keep company. When are you going to come by the house so that you can ask my daddy if you can date his daughter?" she asked with a giggle, even though I knew she was serious. "You have been my boyfriend at school for the past few months, and I would like to see you on the weekends too, ya know?" The smile she gave me at that point was simply a tease. She always smiled like that when she wanted me to kiss her. We would always sneak behind the building and kiss before we went home after school each day, and it was extra-long on Fridays. We didn't go to the same church, so I had to wait until Monday to see her again.

My Mama was grooming me to be a gentleman and not be like that "cheating ass father of mine." She wanted us boys to be respectful and mindful that women liked things to be done a certain way. It wasn't about just getting under a girl's skirt but loving them correctly along the way. I have to admit, in the four and half months that Ava Lynn has been my official "girlfriend," I can say that I do love her.

"Okay Ava, can I come by on Sunday after church and ask your Mama and Daddy if I can keep company with you?" I stared at her very long and hard so that she knew that I was serious.

She nodded her head, yes, and that was that. Now it was time for me to talk to my brothers and Pops to find out exactly what I was supposed to say and do when I got to her house to talk to her parents.

Chapter 4

I woke up to one of the worst sounds I had ever heard - my Mama screaming as if someone just stabbed her in the chest. I leaped from the bed and ran to the front of the house to figure out what was wrong. There was a state trooper standing in the yard. Mama was in a pile on the brick path as my brothers, David and Kevin, both stood tall with tears streaming down their faces. This was definitely not the scene you wanted to wake up to on a cold Saturday morning in January. I ran over to my brothers and asked what was going on. The State Trooper said, "Ma'am, I am so sorry for your loss," turned on his heels and walked out of the yard.

"Can somebody tell me what loss he is sorry for?" I said, shouting at the group.

Kevin looked at me and cleared his throat, "Kenny Boy, Pops died last night." At that moment, my world stopped. The rest of that day was a blur to me. I am not even sure who told my oldest brother, Lester or even Janie Baby, but I know it was not me. The air had been knocked out of my lungs, and I wasn't sure if I would be able to talk again.

As word spread around the county, people started coming over to check on Mama and us kids. It got to be too much for me around late afternoon. I started walking down the road. I just walked and walked and walked. I found myself feeling like the only person that I wanted to talk to was my Ava Lynn. She would know what to say to make this hurt go away.

Ava Lynn lived about ten miles away, close to the school. Wrapped in my own thoughts, it seemed as if in no time I was standing outside of her house. I could hear music coming from one of the rooms in the back of the house, and the light was on. It was pitch-black dark outside, and even though I didn't have on a watch, I knew it was too late to be knocking on a girl's front door. I went around to where the music was coming from, and I could see the girls dancing around in the room.

I had forgotten that it was her birthday and she was having a slumber party. But, I had already made it there, so there was no turning back. I had a piece of paper in my pocket and a pen. Working with Pops, he always made us keep a pen in our pocket and a slip of paper just in case we needed to write something down. I scribbled a note real fast on the slip of paper: *Ava, come outside and meet me behind the broken-down Packard at the end of the property. Love Kendall*

Her window was cracked a little bit so I wrapped my note around a rock, snuck up to the window and tossed it in gently so I knew they would see it, but not be scared and start screaming. After I tossed the rock in, I ran like hell and waited for her to come to me. It was so cold outside that the time that I waited seemed like forever. Aside from being cold, I had such an empty feeling inside of me. It felt like my heart was taken out of my chest, and I did not know what to do. All I knew was that I needed Ava Lynn, my girl. Being with her always made all that was wrong seem right.

I was scared that Mr. Jefferson would find me and shoot me dead in his front yard. I also didn't know if Ava loved me enough to sneak out and come see me. However, the heaviest emotion was sadness. This was the first time that my father was not here to talk to me when I had feelings of uncertainty.

I heard a screaming whisper come from behind me as I looked off into the darkness of the woods across the road. "Kendall Sanford, are you crazy!"

As I turned towards her voice, I could immediately see her body soften; she could tell I had been crying. She kept coming towards me, but now her arms stretched out and hugged me. I melted into her arms, and she just hugged me for as long as I needed. She led me off down a dark path to old man Esau's abandoned barn. He got old, and his kids came and took him up North with them to Chicago. They just let the house and land go. Said they had no use for it because it was so ragged and run down. They just collected their father and walked away from it. The barn was way off the road and behind his old shack so no one could see the light from the lantern that we found.

"So, Kendall, are you going to tell me what this is all about, or are we just going to stay out here in the cold all night and not talk," she said half-jokingly, but with sincere concern in her voice.

I just blurted it out, "My father died today." Having said it aloud seemed to make it real, and oddly enough, a new wave of emotions came over me. We both started to cry, and she hugged me even tighter this time. We hugged for another long while then she pulled back and looked at me as if she were trying to take my pain away. Then she said something she had said many times, but this time, it felt different. "I love you."

I grabbed my Ava in close to me and began to kiss her, and she kissed back with fierceness. I think if you had put a pair of jumper cables on us, you could have jumpstarted a car. That is how intense and powerful that kiss was. Then things started to intensify more. I could not help myself; it was as if things just started happening naturally between us. I felt the roundness of her bottom in the palms of my hands. Then my hands moved up her waist and around to the front of her shirt, and I could feel her nipples stiffen. We slid down to the barn floor, and before I knew it, I could feel the warmth of her insides surrounding me, and we were together in a way that I had only dreamed of up to this point. At this very moment, whatever had happened earlier did not even matter. I knew I loved Ava Lynn, and she loved me. Everything was going to be okay.

Chapter 5

It was warming up slowly in the South. We had a brief winter, but now it was spring, and things were in full bloom. Today was our first day back from Spring Break. It had been over a week since Ava Lynn,and her family left to go visit her relatives in Augusta. I could not wait to see her at school. I had so much to tell her about what I had done over Spring Break. Most importantly, I could not wait to hold her in my arms again.

After that night in the barn, we seemed closer, more in love if that is possible. I guess since it was both of our first times making love, it did something to our souls. It was like we were one. Since that night in the barn, though, we had not been together like that. Not that I didn't want to, because trust me, I wanted to every single time I saw her. We just hadn't done it again.

After the dust settled from Pops funeral and I got my bearings again, I went and asked Mr. and Mrs. Jefferson if it was alright if we could keep company. Every Sunday up until the week before she left for Augusta, I magically appeared on their porch right after I got out of church. I was sixteen and driving one of Pops' trucks, so I had good transportation. We even made plans to go on dates. Her father trusted me enough to take her out when we got back from break. I couldn't wait to see her, but it was taking her forever to get to school that day.

After first period and she was not in class, I started to get a little anxious. I went up to our teacher Mrs. Davis and asked why she had not called Ava Lynn's name when she was checking roll.

"Sweetie, her parents have sent her off to one of those fancy private boarding schools for colored girls," she replied like it was old news. "They announced it at church yesterday and asked the congregation to pray for her while she was away."

Who knew that two boring words like BOARDING and SCHOOL could ruin your entire life? Why didn't she tell me before she left? Did I do something wrong? What the hell was going on? Why would she just leave me and not say goodbye? I was so confused and pissed off that instead of going to my second class, I headed straight to my favorite spot - the pond. I picked up my fishing pole and fished in the pond for the rest of the day.

I met the bus to pick up Janie Mae and walked her home. She wouldn't know if I was on the bus or not because she talked to the little girl in the seat with her then fell fast asleep about the last few miles. I would always have to go wake her up so we could walk home.

When the bus pulled up, my baby sister was true to form. Ms. McQueen let me get on and get her. I told her that I had a doctor's appointment, which was why I wasn't on the bus, and she bought it. "Janie Baby, it's time to go home." She sprung right up, and we were on our way.

That night after dinner, Mama came out on the porch to talk with me. "Son, what is troubling you? Are you missing your Father?"

Since Pops died, any time that we behaved in any unusual manner, she chalked it up to us grieving. She was right in a sense, only I was grieving the loss of my first love.

"No, Mama, just trying to figure some things out. Today I found out that Ava left and went to a boarding school and she did not even say goodbye. Why would she go and do me like that?" I was sad but really mad more than anything else. "Mama, I just can't wrap my head around it. I know she loves me, so why wouldn't she tell me she was leaving?" I was so agitated that my hands were shaking. I was rocking from side to side without even realizing it.

Mama reached over and grabbed my hand to try to calm me. "Baby, there is an old saying that goes something like this: If you love something, let it go. If it returns to ya, it's yours. If it don't, it never was." She sat quietly next to me for a moment as if she was deep in her own thoughts. "Yep, that is what you gotta do. You and your heart gotta let that gal go. If she finds her way back to ya, then you will know for sure." She rocked and looked at me kind of weird. "She was your first love, and first love hurts you like you stepped in a thorn bush when it ends so fast, but trust me, baby. It is plenty other gals out there that will be lucky if you even looks they way." She hugged me, and what she said did make me feel a little better. I began to realize that I would just have to wait for her and see what happens. She had to be back when school let out for summer. I was sure that even boarding schools had a summer break.

A week rolled by and I was still hurt that Ava Lynn just vanished on me. That Sunday, I went out to her parents' house to see if I could get an address to write to her, but no one was home. I went back several weeks in a row, but no one ever answered the door. I finally was fed up and walked around the house to look in the windows.

The house was empty. No furniture was in the rooms, and the walls were bare. As I was walking out of the yard, a truck that was coming down the road slowed down to take a look at me. It was one of Pop's friends who owned the Red Derby, Mr. Buster Tate.

"Little Partna! What you doing out here at Dr. Jefferson's place?" he asked me.

"I was looking for Dr. Jefferson to find out how I could get in touch with Ava Lynn." I figure I had better give full details since it wasn't my property. I didn't know if he could tell I was creeping around looking into windows.

"Oh, well, you know Dr. Jefferson got an offer to work at some fancy hospital up in Augusta. It was out of the blue. He and his wife packed up and had to head out quick-like. They didn't even have time to sell this place before he had to be up there for work. I am actually looking into buying it. Shoot, that is why I crept up so slow. Thought you was someone trying to beat me to it," he said, letting out a hefty laugh. I could tell that laugh was partly because he was being funny, but it was also a sigh of relief that I wasn't gonna be his competition.

"Well, no sir, I didn't know. Thank you for telling me though." I just put my head down, walked back to my truck, and drove home. He was saying something else to me as I walked away, but I could not comprehend anything except the fact that I was never going to find Ava Lynn. Shit! First Pops and then her. I wasn't sure I could stand another loss. Things had to start getting better. I could only hope that Mama was right. I needed to let her go and get her out of my heart, but I wasn't sure exactly how to do it. I saw then that I needed to figure it out real quick, though, or I wasn't ever gonna be happy. David, my brother, got tired of seeing me moping around. He could not understand why I of all people could not get this chick out of my mind. It was summer, and David had just graduated from Bunche High School. "Look at you!" David exclaimed as he walked out to the front porch where I was sitting just looking at the cars ride by along the highway that ran in front of our house. "Man, you let this chick get your nose wide open. That must have been some good horizontal fun for you to be looking like one of these old hunting hounds for the past few months." He chuckled to himself. "I know that you loved her, but you gotta let that go. No chick is worth you missing out on some fun." He plopped down right next to me on the step that I was sitting on. I just looked at him and shook my head. He leaned in a little closer and whispered as if he had the greatest secret that he was about to share with me. "Look, baby bro, the best way to get over one chick is to get another one up under you. You are coming with me to this party, and we gon' find you some new legs to get between."

"It wasn't like that. I loved her, and she loved me. Something happened, and I know that she is going to find her way back to me." I said it, but I couldn't even convince myself that she was really coming back.

"Well, if she really loved you, why she ain't write you yet, huh? Everyone that went to school knows that all you have to do is write a letter, send it to Darien, GA with your name on it and the mailman will find you. It ain't rocket science. She ain't coming back."

I could tell my brother was growing weary with trying to be nice and cheer me up because the next thing he said was, "If you don't get your sad ass up off this front porch! Put your fucking clothes on. We partying tonight, and I don't want to hear two bones about it." So much for being a comfort. David did have a point, though. Why hadn't she tried to reach me by letter? She knew exactly where I was, but I had no clue where she was other than "boarding school." I gathered myself up and went in my room to get myself put together. I knew I wasn't ugly. Hell, I was a Sanford and women basically threw themselves at my brothers (Pops, too, truth be told). I was sixteen and had my whole life ahead of me. Mama was right. After getting cussed out by my brother, I decided it was really time to let her go and see what the night had in store for me.

Chapter 6

It was May of 1958, and the past two years of high school had been a blur. After my big brother got me to stop feeling sorry for myself, I sort of came into my own. While I was wasting time pining away over one woman, there were so many other women that I had yet to conquer.

It was the night of my senior prom, which was a dance that us kids got all dressed up for and took pictures for in the school cafeteria. We did that for about an hour and then went out to the beach, got drunk and partied the night away like every other red-blooded teenage kid in America. I went to the prom without a date because I did not want to be tied down to one girl all night.

Looking around the cafeteria, I have to admit that we cleaned up pretty good for a bunch of "country bunkins." The room was full of all types of dreams, hopes, and aspirations. Most of the kids were going off to colleges like Savannah State, Bethune Cookman, and FAMU and would be heading off to their next stop in life that coming August. Some of the other guys had enlisted into the military.

After my Pops died, my oldest brother, Lester who was back from the war, took over the company, and the business did not miss a beat. Pops was grooming us from the time we were little to take over one day, and his efforts paid off. Kevin was back from completing his business degree at Savannah State College. He had made some connections while there that definitely made business smoother for us. My brother closest to me in age, David, decided long ago that the family business was not for him. He got a football scholarship to a school way up north called Delaware State. He told us that he loved the cold weather and would take that over the Georgia summers any day. Mama and I had been up to see two of his games. His coaches said he was good and might make it to the NFL if he kept playing the way he did. Come graduation, I would not be going off to college or the military. I would be joining my two oldest brothers in the family business of running pulpwood. But that night, I was only concerned with what lucky girls would get to dance with the catch of the county.

After dancing with several girls that had come to the prom alone, I decided that I wanted to try my luck with Cynthia. Her daddy was a preacher at one of the largest churches in McIntosh County, and you know what they say about preachers' daughters. They act all sweet and innocent but act loose if you get them alone.

When the next Sam Cooke song came on, I asked her to dance, and she did not disappoint. She moved all too well to the tune, and her nibbling on my ear, while her head was buried in my shoulder, was enough to let me know that the night was going to end alright.

She left the prom with me that night and was my date to the after-party at the beach. Since Cynthia was a preacher's kid, she still had a curfew even though it was prom. She was not really my date, so I did not feel the pressure to have her home on time. We actually ended up laughing and talking for most of the night. Around midnight she looked up at me with her hazel eyes and said, "Kendall, I have to get ready to head home. I had so much fun with you tonight. When I wasn't asked to the prom by anyone that I wanted to go with, I just knew tonight was going to be a bore. You came and saved me." She looked down at her hands and then back up at me, "I have liked you for a long time. Why haven't you ever asked me out or shown interest in me before tonight?"

Once she said that I knew I was in there. I looked at her with a half-smile, "If you liked me, why didn't you say something to me?"

"Boy! I am a lady, and I do not chase after any man," she said, swatting at my chest.

"Well, I like you, too, Cynthia. Why don't you let me show you how much I like you?" I pulled her in close to me, kissed her softly, and held her tight up against my body. I could feel her relax into my arms, and we twined into one right there on the sand dune. She felt so good I wasn't sure that I could make it last long enough to please her, but before I released, I heard her make a sound that no one had ever made before, and I could feel her body shivering underneath me. I knew this was the first time that I had made a girl climax, and that excited me so much that I released almost at the same time. This girl felt amazing, and she did not know it, but that was exactly how I wanted my night to end.

After the prom, Cynthia and I sort of became an item. We dated for a while, although I still had my other girls that I would see. If the sex wasn't so good, I would have probably not even have bothered with the dating part. It was only so I could get her in the back seat of my truck and make the magic happen. This went on all summer until she saw me with Donna at the diner one Sunday afternoon in August. I figured Cynthia would still be at church at that time, but nope. She walked right into the same diner with one of her girlfriends from church to get a shake. They both walked over to me, and Cynthia slapped me across the face so hard that I could not speak for at least a full minute because of the sting. Then Donna stood up and demanded that I take her home because I had embarrassed her. I lost two girls all in one swoop. Damn! It just wasn't my day.

Chapter 7

You always knew when you were getting close to the paper mills because the funky smell would let you know. Whenever anyone visited Darien, they would always ask about the smell. Local folks would always reply, "Oh, that's just Camp Union." The smell of the mill was just a part of their everyday life, but to my family, that stench meant much more. It meant stability, livelihood, and food on the table. Whenever the mills were running, that meant some of our trucks were making money as well.

It had been two months since the fiasco with Donna and Cynthia at the diner. I told myself that I was just going to lay low and focus on work until I got used to this new way of life. It was hard work, but working for myself was very satisfying to me even if it was a family business and Lester took the role of being in charge since he was the oldest. He couldn't fire me, but I really didn't want to disappoint Mama's or Pops' legacy, so I worked twice as hard to make sure that we were successful.

"Hey, Kenny Boy," my brother, Kevin, said as I walked into the office at the truck yard. "There is a message for you from Donna. She said she needs to talk to you, and it's urgent. She left a number at her school for you to call her."

I looked at him and wondered what she could have possibly wanted. The last time I had seen her was when I dropped her off at home after leaving the diner when I was busted. I picked up the slip of paper that Kevin had scribbled the number on and dialed the numbers to call her. It rang a few times, and then a girl with a very heavy voice, which almost sounded like a man, picked it up.

"Gibbs Hall second floor."

I looked at the paper again and said, "Hello, may I speak with Donna Sanders in room 205, please?" There was a pause and then a knock and yell in the background. "Donna, phone for you."

A few minutes went by as my mind wondered what the dorm at Donna's school must look like. FAMU was about four hours from home. I just knew she was calling to tell me she missed me and wanted me to come visit. I could have gone down, too. I had a cousin I could stay with that lived in Tallahassee. I could have made it work or made her wait until she came home on break to see me. I wasn't sure I even want to be bothered with her, though. She didn't even let me explain about Cynthia. She just cut me off cold turkey. I thought she was through with me.

"Hello?" I heard from a voice on the other end of the phone line.

"Is this Donna?" I asked. The voice did not sound like I remembered.

"Yes, this is me. Is this Kendall?"

"Yeah, it's me, Donna. How ya been? I hate that we ended things the way that we did." She did not say anything, so I continued. "I got your message at work saying you needed to talk to me, and it was real important. What's going on, Donna?"

"Well, Kendall, I'm not quite sure how to tell you this. Umm, well, I just needed to let you know that you gonna be a daddy. I just wanted you to know. I don't need nothing from you. They have housing here for girls like me so we can finish school. So, I'm going to finish school, be a nurse, and move on with life. I just wanted you to know that I have your baby in my belly."

I wasn't sure what to say, but after I said it, I knew immediately that it wasn't the right thing to say. "How you know it's mine? Are you sure you pregnant?"

CLICK!

That had to be the loudest dial tone that I had ever heard in my life. I was 18 years old, and I was going to be a father. What possessed me to ask her that last question? What was I thinking? She must have been scared, and that took a lot of courage to call. It sounded like she had it all figured out. *What do I do now? Should I call her back? Should I drive down there and see her face to face?* I really didn't know what to do. Moments like those I wished my Pops was still around. I decided to go with the next best thing, my older brothers.

Lester, my oldest brother, was twenty-five and married to a girl named Bell, his high school sweetheart. When he got back home from the war, they got married and quickly started a family. Their house was over in Brunswick on some acreage he purchased for them adjacent to some of the land that we grew timber on and forested for the paper mills. He and Bell had my two nieces, Joyce, who was four, and Gail, who was two. They seemed to have it all together. My sister-in-law stayed home and raised the family while my brother ran the family business. I wanted to be exactly like my brother, but Ava disappeared so many years ago. But I had a baby on the way and was just getting started with my life.

After I knocked on the door, Bell came out and opened it with a big smile. "Kenny Boy, what are you doing out this way? I didn't know we was expecting you to stop by. Come on in. I was just about to put supper on the table. You know your brother likes us to all sit down together and eat. Take your jacket and put it over there on the coat rack and come in the kitchen."

"Thanks, sis. Where is Lester? I wanted to talk to him real quick. Wait, is that gumbo I smell?" She smiled and shook her head, yes. She knew that was my favorite with a big piece of cornbread on top. "Well, I guess I am staying for supper then." I went on in and sat down in their front room where the TV was. They had a color set, and I did enjoy watching it when I came to visit. Mama and me still had the old black and white TV. It still worked so Mama said it was no use wasting money on a new one when the old one worked perfectly fine.

I turned to the evening news, and Douglas Edwards was on CBS telling me what all was happening in the world. I heard Bell yell out back towards the horse barn. "Les-tah! Kenny Boy is here! Come on ta da house."

I heard the giggles and squeals from on the other side of the house and in rushed two of the sweetest little people. They jumped on me and started hugging and saying, "Uncle Kenny, do you have quarters for us?"

"For my favorite Sugar Babies, of course, I have something. Let me check my pockets." I reached in my pockets and pulled out two shiny quarters and handed each of my nieces one. They ran off to show their Mama. Just as they left the room, Lester came in.

"Kenny Boy, didn't I just leave you over at the truck yard earlier? What you doing out here at the house? You must have smelled Bell's seafood gumbo," he laughed, jabbing me playfully in the ribs.

"Nah! I just needed to talk to someone about a situation. You know, I just needed to talk to my brother." He got real still.

"This sounds serious. Walk out to the barn with me real quick."

Lester hollered over his shoulder towards the kitchen where Bell was, "I'm taking Kenny Boy out to the barn real quick to show him how good my horses are looking."

"Les-tah, don't you stay out there too long. Supper's about to be on the table. You and Kenny Boy better wash up before you come in my house after being with them animals." Bell was fussing like she was joking, but we both knew how serious she took washing your hands before eating.

We walked out the back door and out to the barn, which was actually cozy on the inside. He had a little table and chairs set up so he could get a moment to himself away from all that estrogen that was floating around in his house when he needed it.

"So, what is going on with you. You aight?"

I stared at the ground for a long while. When I finally looked up, I said, "I'm gone be a daddy."

"Cynthia IS pregnant! I knew it when I saw her at Piggly Wiggly last week. I told Bell I knew that gal was pregnant! She said that I was being insensitive and that she probably was just gaining a little weight."

"No! Donna is pregnant. She called me from school this afternoon and let me know that I was gonna be a daddy."

"So, what are you going to do about it? Is she going to have the baby? What did she say exactly?" He shot questions out at me like a firing squad.

"Man, I don't know. I know I hurt her feelings because she hung up on me."

"What exactly did you say?"

"I asked her how she knew it was mine." I felt so ashamed admitting what I had asked her.

"Damn, I can't imagine what I would have said. She can't really hold that against you because that is a normal question." He cocked his head to the side and said the phrase that all of us knew all too well. "Mama's baby, daddy's maybe."

"I know, man, but that's not me. I know I was with her, and the timing is right. I mean I screwed her about five or six different times, but it only takes once. I gotta make this right."

"What do you mean, make it right? You gonna marry her or ask her to get rid of it? You know Mrs. Bessie makes that potion that makes the girls lose the babies."

"Nah, I ain't doing neither. I just need to make sure she and my baby are okay." I couldn't see marrying her. She was fun to sleep with, but I wasn't considering making her my wife.

"Well, she could have done worse. I mean you do have money, and we are a good family. Just make sure she ain't just after you trying to get a payday is all I am going to say. She might have seen you and saw dollar signs. Just make sure you do it right. Don't put your name on the birth certificate. You can give her some money, but whatever you do, don't put that baby in your name."

Lester and I finished our talk and went inside to chow down on some gumbo that my sister-in-law cooked. It was good to have my big brothers to talk things through with me. Family keeps me grounded and even if they tell you things you might not want to hear about yourself sometimes, it is important to listen, take in what they are saying, and see what you can do to best fit you. It is funny like that sometimes. I don't think that Donna was after money. I just got caught with my pants down, literally.

Friday night after work, I had made up in my mind to drive to Florida and see Donna. I hadn't tried to call her back since she told me that she was pregnant and hung up the phone because of that stupid question that I had asked her. I thought to myself, *you gotta go make this right and you gotta do it in person.* My plan was to get up before daylight in the morning and take the drive to see her.

I drove home from the truck yard and was mapping out what I would say when I saw her. A big truck was parked alongside the road near the house. As I pulled into the yard, I could see Mama standing on the porch talking to someone. I parked my truck, got out, and walked towards the front of the house to see what was going on. It was Bishop Williams, who was tall in stature and strong in build. He used to box and still did occasionally between preaching the Word of God.

I walked up and hugged Mama then shook the Bishop's hand and started. "Hi, Bishop. What brings you out this way this evening?"

He looked at Mama and tipped his hat, "Flora, it was good seeing you. Do you mind if I talk with your son man to man in private out here?"

"You sure I can't interest you in a cold beverage, Bishop? I also have a potato pie if you would like a piece," Mama said. She exuded the core essence of southern hospitality.

"No, thank you. I want to talk to this young man then I will be on my way."

Mama went into the house, and the Bishop and I both took seats in the rocking chairs that Mama had lining the porch wall.

I started because I felt like I needed to get a jump on this joker. I felt like he wanted something, but I was not sure what it was. "Bishop, what can I help you with this evening, sir? It has been a long time since I've seen you and Mrs. Williams since Cynthia broke up with me and all." I added that last piece so he would know that she left me.

"Kendall, Cynthia is a good girl from a good family. In my church, there are certain beliefs that we hold, and one of them is that sex before marriage is frowned upon. You and my daughter seemed to have forgone that notion, and I know this because right now, she is starting to get heavy with your baby. Now, son, I came here to talk to you about how you are going to make this right. I have thought long and hard about this. I know that you two loved each other, and I understand that you got caught with another girl, which is why my daughter stopped dating you." He paused, waiting for me to say something, but at this particular moment, whatever power I thought I created by starting the conversation had exited my body so swiftly that it left no remnant behind. He continued, "You two need to be married so that this baby is not an abomination to the Lord. I knew your father, and I know that he raised you to be a man and take on your responsibilities as such. I expect you to make this right and make an honest woman out of my daughter. Marry her before this thing gets outta hand."

I still sat stunned at what I was hearing. The Bishop left and said that he expected to see me at his house tomorrow at noon for the ceremony. He already had it planned out, and everything was in place. Bishop probably was thinking it was all about Cynthia when actually I had

Donna on my mind. How in the fuck did I get two girls pregnant all at the same time? This was something you only heard about. It shouldn't have happened to someone like me. Now my plans for Saturday were to go see Donna and make it right. But I had just found out that I had to make it right with Cynthia, too.

I finally fell asleep after my mind was racing all night long. I had decided that I was just gonna go to Donna instead of Bishop's house at noon. Making it right that way wasn't my exact idea of making it right. I went outside to get something from my truck and guess who was sitting out by the road? That same truck that was out there last night when I got home from work.

"Good morning, Kendall. I stopped by just to remind you that you have an appointment at noon. I suppose that you ain't thinking of not showing up, are you?" He looked down at me with a scowl that said, "Nigger, I wish you would." I could also see that the Bishop came with some backup. I had heard of shotgun weddings, but I was about to be a part of one in a few short hours.

"Morning Bishop. Nah, I heard you loud and clear yesterday, and I plan to make it right with Cynt." I am not sure of how convincing that sounded to him, but it was all I could muster up.

"Good. Well, I am here to escort you just to make sure." The Bishop was serious, and I knew that he was only doing what was best for his daughter and their family reputation. This is what I get for dating a preacher's daughter. I promised him and his wife that I would mind myself while dating her and look what happened. Well, I guess what he said about my father was correct. I had to face this responsibility like a man. I was going to be a husband and a father all before my twenty-first birthday.

After I told Mama what was going on, she agreed and said that if I laid down, then I needed to make up the bed. I neglected to tell her about Donna. How was I supposed to make up two beds? This one was gonna have to do for now. She followed us over to the Bishop's house where we were united in holy matrimony. Although I had not seen her in months, Cynthia did look beautiful standing in that gown. I could see why my brother said he thought she was pregnant. Her face had gotten really round and her belly, though not big yet, was sticking out a little.

When the Bishop said that he had everything already arranged, he really did. He had the marriage certificates printed up already, the outfits for both of us to wear so that the pictures came out nice, and a place for us to live. He bought a small place out on some land and had it made ready for us to move in right after the "wedding."

That house was probably the best part of the deal. That place was so nice, and I enjoyed everything about it. My new father-in-law, in what my best guess was a gesture meant as a peace offering for forcing me to marry his daughter, had these twenty acres put in my name. I know because when my brother told me to check the land deed at the county office, sure enough, it had my name and my name only listed. I tried to ask him about it one day and thank him. He brushed it off and said something to the effect of family takes care of family. The catch to it was that three acres that the homestead was on and the house were in Cynthia's name. Bishop was generous, not crazy. I guess he figured that if I ever started catting around with other women, Cynt could put me out and still have a home for her and the baby.

The months after we were married rolled by quickly, and Cynt got bigger and bigger with the baby every day. I was glad that I got to see the baby growing like this. It made me wonder what it would look like. Would it be a boy or girl? Would I ever be as good of a father to this baby as Pops was to me? My mind would also wander down to Tallahassee. Was Donna growing like this, too?

It was a Wednesday afternoon when I got a call at work that I was a daddy. I rushed home, and there were some cars in the yard when I pulled up. Cynthia's family members had stopped by to check on her and the new addition to the family.

I walked into the bedroom where they were, and Cynthia lay awake with her mother and aunt stationed on the side of the bed. She looked up at me and said, "Come in and meet your son."

My son! I was really a daddy. "Hello, there little fella," I said. I was not comfortable enough to pick up anything that small, so I just watched him as he slept.

My mother-in-law chimed in quick. "Meet Wilson Thurmond Sanford. Cynthia is naming that boy after her daddy."

I was not sure what came over me, but I reached down, grabbed my son from the bed, and pulled him in close to me. "No, Claudette. This here is Kendall Sanford, Jr. This is my son, and he will have my name."

From that moment on, we had a name for the baby. My son. My namesake.

Kendall Jr. was about a month old when I found myself in the Florida A&M University hospital. Donna had her baby and sent a message that I was a daddy yet again. It was scary how much this baby looked like his older brother. When I visited with Donna, she seemed at peace with how things were going. I could tell she was going to be a great mother, and this little guy had two parents that were going to love him no matter what. When she asked me what his name should be, I told her that since I already had a Kendall that his name should be Kenneth Nathaniel Sanford. His eyes were a gray-blue, just like Pops. After seeing him, I knew he was definitely mine. I went against my brother's advice and gave him my last name. I spent the night on the hospital chair and drove them home to Donna's place before I left to head back to my family in Darien.

"Kendall, thank you for coming to see us," Donna said to me with a hint of sadness in her voice.

"I had to come see my son. I know that my actions and words with you have not really been the best choices, but, Donna, I take care of my responsibilities." I grabbed her hand and continued. "If you ever need anything just reach out, and I will get you taken care of. This is definitely not the ideal situation, but Kenneth will have all of his needs, and most of his wants met. I don't have all of the answers, but we will work through this. I am married now, but she will have to understand that he is going to be in my life."

She smiled a half-smile at me. Of course, right now, these were all just words, and nothing brings power to a man's word more than his actions. When I left, I had already planned to leave some money with her. I knew she was prideful and wanted to prove to me that she didn't need me, so I left a wad of twenty-dollar bills that amounted to five hundred dollars on her kitchen counter. I also took a detour by the school's office to see about the rent for the apartment that she and Kenneth were in. They told me how much it was, and I paid her rent through the end of the next school term. She told me that she would have to go to summer school to catch up on what she missed while she was out this spring having the baby. That was one less thing that she would have to worry about. Room and board was what the lady in the office called it. Whatever it was, it was paid, so I knew that my son had a safe place to live and food to eat.

Then I had to go home and face my wife and tell her that she was not only a mother but a stepmother, too.

When I got home, the house was still dark, so I guess they had not gotten back from revival up in Alabama. Bishop had been asked to preach at a revival because his works in town had gotten him noticed by some important folks that were a part of the Civil Rights movement. Cynthia, being the daddy's girl that she was, would not be left behind even if she wasn't completely healed from having the baby. She said her Mama would be right there alongside her, and that she and Junior would be just fine, which in the end worked out for me, so I didn't have to tell her why I had not been home for so many days. I wasn't real sure how she was going to take it that I had another son that could be Junior's twin, not only in looks but age too since they were just a month apart.

It looked like I got back just in time. There were not any signs of them anywhere in the house, so the coast was clear. I was tired, so I washed up and went to bed. When I had a lot of stuff on my mind, the things that I thought about tended to keep me awake. With everything that was going on, I was surprised that I fell right to sleep. It did not last long, though. About midnight, the lights popped on, and Cynthia came into the room. Her parents had dropped her and Junior off and where headed home. Traveling while being Negro in the South meant you had to drive straight through most times because hotels and restaurants did not service you. There was that little green book, but most times that took a lot of work to map things out.

My father-in-law was also very prideful. He wanted to prove that he could drive for however many hours straight without needing to utilize the white man's anything. If they did not want him in there, then he certainly was not going to use their second rate nothing. He would rather piss in the woods alongside the road than to ask them for anything. If he didn't have to stop at the fill-up station, he wouldn't, but every car needs gas, so pride had to take a back seat for that little while or he wouldn't be able to make it home.

Cynthia breezed in, kissed me on the lips, and handed me the baby while she went to the bathroom. I was groggy, but I had missed this little man. I did not mind waking up to see his hazel eyes. *Yep, you and your little brother are going to be hell on the girls when you grow up.* Two good-looking Sanford boys. It was real to me, two sons all within a few weeks of each other. Well, I wasn't gonna bother Cynthia with the details about any of that right then. I decided to just wait until the morning.

The next morning, I woke up to the smell of pan-fried bacon. One luxury about marrying Cynt was the girl could burn in the kitchen. It was Saturday, so I had planned to rest up, and possibly get put out to sleep on the land once Cynt found out I fathered another child.

I walked down the hallway to the kitchen, and she looked so good standing in her nightgown. I forgot that I needed to tell her something.

I walked up behind her, grabbed her behind, and kissed her on the neck. "Good morning, wife." She swatted at me and told me to let her finish cooking.

"Where's Junior?"

"He is in the crib in his room, why?"

"Well, I missed my wife all week. I want you right here in this kitchen."

She rolled her eyes, but she turned the fire on the stove off. Then we both turned the fire between us up to high. Since we had been married, we had reconciled and actually started to fall in love with each other. Once we made love that first time, we had been like rabbits until the day Junior was born. Now to see her in her nightgown with her titties so full and peeking at me through that see-through white cotton was enough to drive a man wild. She lost most of the baby weight, and the little that she had left was hitting her in all the right places. She had me turned on that morning, and we both knew it was time to get back to being newlyweds.

We had a deep freezer in the back corner of our kitchen. I bent her over, and we both came on home. She was moaning so loud I thought that something was hurting her, but she told me I had better not stop. So, I didn't. Let's just say we had dessert before breakfast that morning.

Once we got ourselves together and cleaned up, Cynthia finished cooking breakfast, and we sat down to eat. Junior was still asleep, so I figured now was as good a time as any.

"Cynt, you know that I take being married to you very serious, right?" She just nodded her head yes and continued eating her breakfast. I went on, "There is something that I need to tell you. Do you remember when we stopped dating last summer because you caught me in the diner with Donna? Well, when you left, I got a call that Donna had a baby boy, and he is mine. While you were gone with your parents to Alabama, I went to visit her and the baby-- his name is

45

Kenneth -- at the hospital. He looks just like Kendall Jr." She put her fork down and continued to chew her food. Then she started slowly.

"I had heard that your little bitch was pregnant, and I had a feeling it was yours. You know that her family goes to our church. How is this going to look when she bounces back here with a baby the same age as mine with the same last name as mine, but he ain't mine? You are determined to embarrass me, aren't you? We met a year ago, and we have dated, broke up because you ran around on me, found out I was pregnant, got married, HAD the baby, and now I find out the person you cheated on me with has a baby, too. Damn!" She pushed back from the table quickly. "How did I get involved in something like this?" I think she was asking this of herself, so I didn't answer. I let her finish, "I need to go get my baby up and get ready for the day. Enjoy the rest of your breakfast, husband."

That was it. She wasn't really mad. She was just embarrassed. That exchange went much better than I imagined that it would. I just knew it would end with me sleeping out in the shed I built behind the house last month. I need to remember that for next time I have some bad news to deliver. Fuck her real good before I drop a bomb on her.

We walked around the house, silent for hours. I finally went outside to work in my garden. This was mostly to get out of the house but still be at home. After the day faded into evening and we sat at the table for another meal together again. I could tell that she wanted to talk to me, but that stubbornness would not allow her to go first. Therefore, I figured I would let her off the hook, and I started the conversation.

"Junior has been doing better with sleeping. You not getting up as much as you was the first few weeks." Whenever I talked about the baby, she always responded.

"Yeah, he's getting better about sleeping longer. Mama said that babies generally will get on the schedule of the outside world. It just takes them a little while to adjust. Until then, we on his time." She had a smile on her face. Talking about him has a way of doing that to her. I

46

saw the same thing when I was with Donna and Kenneth for that short time. I guess it is something that all mothers have built inside of them.

"Yeah. That is true. He sure does have all of his mama's attention. His daddy can get a little jealous, you know? I want some of mama's attention, too." I got up and slid around the table so that I was able to embrace her. "Most importantly, Cynt, I want you to know that we will be alright. No matter what happens, I am here with you and Junior. I know that we will have to figure this out now that Kenneth is born, but I am sure there is a way to make this work without getting you all worked up. We got a lifetime to get through together, so what can I do as your husband to make you smile?" When I said this, I lifted her chin and kissed her very softly. She did not respond initially, but she could not resist me. We ended the day how it started, and all was well in the Sanford household. At least for that moment, anyway.

Chapter 8

"The numbers from our trucks running to Savannah look great, guys. Our Brunswick numbers are looking good, too. We are closing in on one of our most profitable years yet. We need to make sure that we are planting our forest out in Charlton, Camden, and Ware on time. Rotating harvest so that we can keep a steady flow of wood so that our trucks are running our trees to the mills. Our Wayne and Brantley County forests are ready for harvest. I've gotta give it to you guys – Kevin, you were right about us getting into foresting. And Kendall? You were spot on finding us the land for the prices that we got it for. This is what Pops wanted for us. To be successful and make a way in this world on our own terms. Even though David is a big shot in the NFL and hasn't joined us yet! Let me say it like this. He might still come around and get into the family business. We are realizing his dream."

My older brother, Lester, leaned forward on the desk in the office as he was wrapping up our business meeting. We had meetings with the executive board, which is my two brothers and me, once a month just to make sure we are all focused and on the same page. Kevin spent most of his time in our Savannah office, and Lester opened an office in Brunswick. I worked out of the Darien office, which was our original site. Cynthia came in and actually decorated an area for me so that I had a nice place just like my older brothers. I like the ruggedness of the truck yard though. It somehow made me feel closer to my Pops. We also had our meetings in Darien because it was the heartbeat of our business, and all of us were responsible for making sure that we kept our family legacy going.

"Now that business is out of the way. What is going on with my brothers?" Kevin asked us as he reached for a glass and poured up some brandy. A toast with the brothers was a new ritual that we had recently added to our meetings. I think after Kevin had a meeting with some white businessmen and they did it, he decided we should too. Lester and I did not mind at all.

"Well, you guys are going to be uncles again," Lester said with a huge grin across his face. "Y'all pray it's a boy this time. I really want a son, and I want to help carry on the family name. Kenny Boy, you can't corner the market on that for all of us."

"Yeah, Kenny Boy! Now that Donna is back from school, what is happening with that?" Kevin chimed in.

"Well, I take care of what is mine. If that means Donna gets something out of it too, then it just is what it is. I bought a place for her out on Route 59. It has about two acres and a house just big enough for them both. I put a fishing pond at the house too so I could have a place to take the boys fishing together. " My brothers looked back and forth between each other, then back at me. "

"What does Cynt have to say about this? I mean does she know that Donna is back, and you are keeping her in a house that is right down the road from you and Cynthia's house?" Lester was always concerned that Cynthia was going to snap on me one day, even though I explained to him that she understands and is not bothered by me helping raise my son.

"All I know is Bell would have shot my ass by now." Lester started laughing, and Kevin joined in cracking up.

Kevin stopped and added, "Kenny Boy, we all know you still fucking Donna on a regular. Ain't no way Cynt don't know. You mean to tell me that when you would go to Florida, Cynthia did not get mad? Now you got her a house near you, and she don't care at all? Shit, I know you a Sanford man and all, but damn. What the hell? You must have put some voodoo on them or something."

"Look! Alright, yeah, I'll admit it. Donna and me, we have been together. And well, yeah, she is good to me. I can't lie. I'm married to Cynthia, so we have that special thing between us. She just gets me and doesn't give me any grief." As I said it, it did sound crazy, but it was the truth.

"Well don't fuck around and get killed having two households. I can see the headline now: Nigger gets shot by his woman for keeping his bastard child's mother happy."

"Kenneth ain't no bastard. Say it again, Kevin and see won't it be the last thing you utter on this earth."

"You right. I'm sorry. You know I love my nephews -- both of them just the same. I went too far, but you gotta be real and admit that is what it looks like." Kevin stopped the laughter because he could see that I was growing angry.

"Let's focus on something more important. Janie Mae is a freshman at Bunche this year, and we need to make sure that Mama has all the help she needs to keep these little knuckleheaded boys away from our baby sister," Lester stated, changing the subject altogether. If it was one thing that we could all agree on, it was our baby sister was to be taken care of. She was the absolute jewel of the family.

"Lester, we are always around, and she is a good kid. Janie Mae is going to be okay," Kevin chimed in.

"I just want to make sure that we are all doing whatever we can to help Mama, and make sure they are taken care of, okay?" Lester added, although this was already understood.

Mama let us run the business as we saw fit, but she was also an owner. She always got her profit share first, and Janie Mae's went into a trust fund as well as a college tuition fund. Kevin picked up on how to be a good financial planner in business school, and he was going to make sure that our family would be fine in the event of a financial crisis. He made us all invest and save. Even if we protested, we knew he was right. Live off what you need and put the rest away for a rainy day.

"I make a motion to adjourn this Sanford Brothers Pulpwood Company meeting. Do I hear a second?" I asked because I was ready for my brothers to head out.

Kevin spoke up, "I second that motion."

"Meeting adjourned!" Lester said, officially closing us out.

I had to stop by and make sure Donna and Kenneth were doing okay before heading home. We needed to start heading out so that I could be home in time for dinner.

"You are looking at the first and the only negro registered nurse of the McIntosh County General Hospital," Donna exclaimed as I walked into the house. She was spinning around, and I could tell that she was excited to share this news with someone.

"Wow! Congratulations! You are going to be the best nurse this hospital has ever seen," I replied.

"This calls for a toast." I walked to the kitchen to look for glasses and some drinks.

"I can't believe it. Here I am beating the odds and making history," she continued with her excitement. "Kendall, you don't know how many days I felt like giving up, but I refused to end up back at home working at the oyster factory. I did it! I graduated, passed my nursing exams, and now look at me. I've got my first nursing job, and I am breaking barriers for other colored nurses. You know what they say. Once one of us is in, the rest will soon follow."

Donna was so happy she did not even realize that I was in her personal space. When she moved back, she made it clear that it was strictly about Kenneth. I was another woman's husband, and she could not carry on with me like we had when I would visit her while she was at school. I handed her the glass and began to make a toast.

"Here is to one of the smartest women I have ever met, who will make her family, the entire colored community of Darien, her son, and his father very proud. I love you, Donna. Congratulations! You deserve this, baby." We both took a sip of the brown liquid and enjoyed Donna's moment.

After I didn't see him for a while, I finally asked, "Where is Kenneth? He usually would have come in by now if he was off playing somewhere."

"Oh, he is over with his grandparents. Daddy was taking him to some auction or another tonight with him. They had some hogs to sell."

"Well, I guess I have invaded your space for long enough. I better get on down the road and get home in time for supper," I said as I walked back in the kitchen to put up the dirty glasses. "Congratulations, again. You really are making all of us proud. You are making me proud."

"Kendall, do I really make you proud?" She stared at me as if she was in disbelief.

"Yeah! You are doing things despite the circumstances. Most women would have had an abortion or given up on school. You did what was right and what was important to make a life for yourself. You are an amazing mother, and you know I love you." As I said that last statement, I ran my hands down her arms. "You are so smart and beautiful, Donna." I couldn't believe that I was still this close to her, and she hadn't pushed me away yet. "I am glad that you are still in my life."

Donna pulled me into her, and we started to kiss. After a few moments, I pulled away and asked her, "Are you sure you want to do this?" Her body immediately told me yes. I was glad Kenneth wasn't home so we could just get to it right there in the living room. Donna was so different from Cynthia in her movements and the way that her body felt in my hands.

This was unreal. I thought we were done, but I guess the liquor and the moment let her forget about my wife, who was less than two miles down the road. We were both butt ass naked in the middle of the living room. I laid down on the floor and Donna rode me like a cowgirl on one of those bucking horses that you see at the county fair. Man, this woman was giving me all that she had, and I was not complaining one bit. That evening we did some things that house had probably never seen before. When we both finished, we went into the bedroom to recuperate.

"Kendall, what made you choose Cynthia and her baby over us?"

"Is that what you think I did?" I rolled her towards me and held her in my arms. "Baby, me and you is not ideal or what you wanted. We are here now, though, and I promise you that I am going to take care of you both. I have lived up to my promise of that so far, haven't I?"

She shook her head, yes, and I could tell that this had been bothering her because her eyes started to tear up.

"Donna, don't cry, baby. I am here." As I said it, I realized that I was going to have to leave and go home soon. For right now, I had to comfort her and make sure that she was all right.

Once Donna fell into a deep sleep, I knew she was out because she was snoring lightly. I washed up in the bathroom and headed down the road to my house, which I shared with my wife and our son.

Chapter 9

I promised Cynthia that I would take her to Savannah to go Christmas shopping. They had more stores and a better selection, according to her. I couldn't have cared less about the holiday or shopping, but this is what she wanted to do so I drove her up Highway 17 into the city.

Broughton Street was lined with shops, but over the years, many of them had closed down. The few that were left were still much more than what we had in Darien, so the drive was well worth it. She went from store to store, and at about the fifth store, I told her that I would just meet her back in front of the Globe shoe store at 2:00 pm.

Junior and Kenneth were spending time at their Uncle Kevin's house so that we could get some shopping done, and Santa could still be part of their childhood. I was thinking about making that the last year that Santa might visit. The boys were nine and starting to question that story. James Brown's song *Santa Claus Go Straight to the Ghetto* rekindled that Christmas fire for both boys, but we were not too certain how long it would last.

Cynthia said she wasn't hungry and wanted to continue shopping. However, I was getting hungry, and I had passed my tolerance for shopping two stores ago. My brother, Kevin, and his wife, Lou (short for Louvenia), had taken me to a restaurant that had some really good food. It wasn't far away from Broughton Street, and if my memory served me, it was called Mrs. Wilkes. I hopped in my pickup truck and drove over to get me some lunch.

By the time I was done eating, I had a belly full of the best fried chicken, greens, and cornbread that anyone could find. The people who were next to me were fun, and I could tell that some of the ladies were not sure if I was or was not a Negro, so my smiles met some of theirs with uncertainty, which was all right as long as I got my stomach full. My Uncle Bill had a saying. "A stomach full ain't nothing but a stomach full," but when it's full of some good food, that makes it twice as nice.

As I walked down the azalea-lined sidewalk back to my car, I could not believe my eyes. It couldn't be her. Even after twelve years, I was almost positive that it was Ava Lynn walking towards me on this sidewalk in Savannah, GA. She was looking down at her watch, and I could tell she hadn't noticed me yet. Before I could stop myself, my voice took over before my brain could process what I was about to do.

"Ava Lynn Jefferson, is it really you?" I asked with a boom.

She looked up at me as if she had seen a ghost. Her face got pale, and she looked at me with disgust. She finally said something that surprised both of us.

"Yeah, it's me." She barked that out as if it was a warning to stay away from her. I obviously did not care because my brain reverted to being that sixteen-year-old that was in love with this very girl who seemed pissed at the sight of me.

"Ava, why you so cold? I can't believe it's you. After you left and went off to boarding school...I just can't believe it's you standing here in front of me. I wondered what I would say to you if I ever saw you again. I have so many questions, but..."

She put her hand up to stop me from speaking. "Kendall Sanford, I can't believe that you have the balls to stand here and act like you didn't hurt me."

Now I was totally confused and actually growing irritated, so I asked, "How did I hurt you, Ava when you were the one to up and leave and go to only God knows where? My life was turned upside down because you left me without any explanation right after I lost my Pops. You knew I was still hurting, and then to lose you on top of it... It was almost too much for me."

She got this look on her face that was a little softer than the initial scowl but was now more curious.

"Why are you pretending like you don't know where I went, and why I left Darien?"

"Ava Lynn, this is not fake. Up until this moment, I had no clue if you were dead or alive. It took me a long time to get past the fact that you were not coming back to me. Right now, I feel like I am looking at one of the biggest holes from my past straight in the face, and I don't know what to do." I was feeling raw and numb all at the same time. How could she affect me like this after all this time?

"Kendall, didn't my parents talk to you. Didn't they tell you where I was?"

"No. I went by your house for weeks, and no one ever answered my knocks. A teacher told me that you had got sent off to boarding school, and Mr. Tate told me that your dad had a new job in Augusta, so he packed up the house and moved." I looked down at my feet then back up at her, "You just vanished without a word." My hurt would not let me not say the next thing. "And you knew exactly where I was, but I never got a letter or nothing. Shit, you could've sent some smoke signals up. I guess I was not fancy enough for the good doctor's daughter. You had to be tucked away from me at that boarding school."

Yep, my feelings were out there. I was sounding like a real punk, but I didn't know if after that day I would ever see her again or get the chance to tell her how fucked up it was the way that she left me.

"Are you saying that you NEVER spoke to either of my parents about where I was?"

"Didn't I just say that? Why do you keep asking me that?" I was pissed all over again as if this was sophomore year in high school. I don't know why she couldn't she get it through her head that I did not know where she was.

She looked at me with those same eyes that she had the night I went to her house when she left her slumber party to be with me. She looked around and then asked me if I would walk with her so we could talk somewhere. We found ourselves at one of the famous parks, Chatham Square, on a park bench. She took a deep breath and began to run down the story of why she had seemingly disappeared.

Turns out that she was pregnant by me. When her parents realized it while they were in Augusta during spring break, they took her over to Boggs Academy, which was a school for pregnant teens. She had actually been pregnant with twins. When it was time for the babies to come bursting into this world, they both were stillborn. I could see the pain in her eyes as she told me, and it pierced my heart because I should have been there for her. Her parents had told her that when they told me that she was pregnant, I denied that I was the father. She did not write to me because she was hurt that I would treat her that way. So, she left Boggs baby-less, finished high school in Augusta, and that was it for her and me.

"So, we have spent over a decade apart, hating each other because of a lie." I was astonished. I heard the cathedral clock chime, and I realized that I was going to be late meeting Cynthia. "Ava Lynn, I have to go, but is there a way that I can get in touch with you? I want to hear more and catch up with you."

"Well, you could always call me. Let me write my number down for you." She reached in her purse to get a piece of paper and pen to write her number down. I took the paper and ran off to my truck to head back over to Broughton Street to meet Cynthia.

Just like that, my past reappeared right before my eyes. We did not have time to talk about what was going on in our current lives. All I knew was that there was a feeling that showed up when I saw Ava Lynn that hadn't been present since I last saw her twelve years ago. I looked at the number and memorized it. I did not want to risk losing that slip of paper or losing her again.

***

When I caught up with Cynthia, I was only five minutes late, so I blamed it on not being able to find a good parking spot. We went by Kevin's house, picked up the boys, and then headed home. The whole drive was filled with Junior and Kenneth telling us all about what they did with Uncle Kevin and their cousins. I was happy that Donna and Cynthia did not mind the boys spending time together. Most folks could not understand our arrangement, but it worked for us. At the age of 29, I had two women I loved, who both had sons I loved, and all of them loved me right back. It was certainly unconventional, but we made it work. Kenneth calls Cynthia, Ma Cynt and Kendall calls Donna, Momma Don. Most people's reactions were either to hold me up on a pedestal as a pimp or shun me as a heathen. Either way, what other people thought of me never really mattered much in my book anyway. I had to work on it with Cynthia because she and her family grew up in the church and always had to keep up appearances. To keep the peace, Donna changed churches, and we just didn't talk about it when we were around Cynthia's people.

That night when we got back home, I was present with my family, but my mind was still back in Savannah where I had seen Ava. So many questions were whirling around in my head about her life. In those few moments, I had only learned of how we were separated, but what about after that? Where did she go to college if she went to college? How many kids did she have? Where did she live? Then the scariest one of them all hit me. Was the true love of my life married to someone else?

I neglected to tell her about my wife. Maybe she had a husband that she did not mention either. I wanted to know more about her. I thought about driving out to my office to call her, but I had no logical reason to give Cynthia for leaving the house that late at night. It would be pushing it to call from the phone at our house. Cynthia was fine with Donna and me because she could reason that since we had a child together, I did have to talk to her sometimes. If she knew I was calling another woman, I don't think that would go so well at the Sanford household. I just stayed there, lying in my bed staring at the ceiling, hoping that my mind would stop racing so that I could hurry up and fall asleep. Tomorrow would be a new day, and I would be able to slip away and call my Ava.

It was crazy how I hadn't seen her in all of that time, but the instant that I saw her, all of those old feelings came rushing back. After I finally fell asleep last night, I did come to a calm about the situation. She had turned back up, and I couldn't let her slip off into the abyss of nowhere again. It was Sunday, which meant a full day of church and family dinner with my in-laws. I went along with my day, but I had already made up in my mind that I was calling Ava first chance I got on Monday morning.

The term *a month of Sundays* is exactly what this particular Sunday felt like. It was the longest day EVER. With the help of some good food and spending time with my two boys, I enjoyed the day. My mind would periodically drift back to that park bench in Savannah where I had reconnected with a ghost from my past.

When I dropped Kenneth off that evening, I could tell Donna wanted some attention. After Kenneth was sound asleep, I put her to bed, too. It was not my best performance, but she knocked out so it must have been alright for her. Honestly, halfway through, I started imagining that she was Ava, and soon after that, I was done. She was asleep, and it was about ten o'clock. I washed up and went back home.

When day broke on Monday morning, it was just like the start of any other week, except I had an extra pep in my step. I knew that I might hear my sweet Ava's voice again. I hated that I couldn't control my excitement. Junior asked me as I was dropping him and his brother off at school if I was okay because I was acting *too* happy. I just hit him playfully on the back of the head, waved good-bye to them both, and headed off to the truck yard.

"What ya say, Kenny Boy?" I saw a cloud of smoke coming from Charlie, one of our drivers that had been with us since before I can remember.

"Nothing, Mister Charlie. How is Sweetie doing these days?" I asked wondering how his wife had been since they found out she has what the old people call the consumption.

"She still hanging on in there. She coughing real bad and seem like she can't hardly catch her breath. I never knew it was going to be this hard watching someone you love slip away from you cough by cough." His whole face turned sad looking as soon as he said it. I could see he was hurting, but there was not a thing anyone could do to take his pain away.

"The doctor gave her less than a month to live. My girls are at the house with they Mama. I can't watch her die. It's just too much for this old fella ta' stand." He didn't look at me. He just stared off into the truck yard as he walked away.

The closest person to me that ever died was Pops, and I did not get to see him. It was just all of a sudden. I couldn't imagine what it must be like to have to watch the woman you love suffer and not be able to help her in any way. I thought about Cynthia and Donna. I do love both of them very much, and I could not imagine watching either of them slip away from me as Sweetie was slipping away from Mister Charlie. Then it slapped me like a ton of bricks. AVA LYNN! I lost her once, and that was a serious pain. I needed to call her to get some much-needed answers about what I missed over the time since we last saw each other. I said a quick prayer for Sweetie and Mister Charlie, then went about my business of the day starting with calling my Ava.

After the second ring, a husky voice said, "Hello, this is Western Sizzler Steak House."

My heart stopped for a moment after hearing a man's voice. When I processed that this was a restaurant, I was able to speak again. "Hello is Ava Lynn Jefferson available?"

"Nobody here by that name."

"Is this 555-4252?" I asked, hoping she had not given me the wrong number.

"Naw! This number is 4253." *CLICK!*

I guess I had wasted enough of his time. Looking at the keypad, I was careful this time to make sure that I dialed the correct number. The phone rang about four times then someone finally picked up.

"Hello, Stevens Residence." The person on the other end of the phone sounded like a white woman.

"Hello, is Ava Lynn Jefferson available?" I asked almost knowing that this had to be a wrong number, too.

"This is she."

"Hi, Ava! It's Kendall. Sorry to call so early in the morning. Are you busy?"

"Hello, Kendall. How are you doing? I was wondering if you were going to call me or not. The way that you ran off the other day left me wondering."

"Sorry about that. I was not really expecting to see you, and then we started talking and time just got away from me. That's all." I was hoping that she didn't ask why I had run off so fast. I was not ready to tell her all about my family just yet. I needed to hear all about her first. I decided that the best way to do that was to plan to talk to her face to face so that I could control everything.

"Ava, I wanted to see if you would be free on Thursday for lunch. I will be in Savannah on business, and it would be great if we could sit down and catch up. That short time when we ran into each other two days ago was not long enough. Plus, I want to see your eyes again. I had forgotten how beautiful they were."

Complementing a woman on her looks was usually a way to seal the deal, in most cases. My grandfather once told me if you want a girl to like you, there was one surefire line. Look at her straight in the eye and say, "Girl, you shole is cute." After he told me that, I thought he was just an old player that didn't know anything about women, but I be damned if it didn't work every single time. I will never forget that piece of advice. Matter of fact, I had already passed it down to my two boys.

She responded, "Thursday will be good. Where do you want me to meet you?"

"Meet me at the Rib Hut on Bay Street at noon. I plan to be done with my morning meetings by then and will meet you there."

"Alright. I know where that is, and I love their food. See you soon. Goodbye, Kendall."

"Bye, Ava. See you Thursday."

My business meeting was not a true meeting. I normally met up with Kevin to give a rundown of the week's happenings, drop off any paperwork for payments of the guys, and pick up checks. We each had our own offices and areas of the business to maintain, and Kevin handled all the monetary matters. He was good at it, so we let him take care of everything. Since this was a normal work trip for me, neither Cynthia nor Donna would think much of me heading up the highway to Savannah.

The days between Monday and Wednesday were a blur. I know I was screwing Cynthia one night and Donna the next, but with both of them, Ava Lynn would enter my mind, and I would immediately release. As much as both of my women liked to screw, I can't believe neither of them had been pregnant again. I guess that was a good thing.

I left out before daybreak headed to the Savannah office. When I got there, our meeting ran the same as it usually did. I was glad that Kevin and Lester both had things to do afterward so that I didn't have to explain why I wasn't going to eat lunch with them.

As I came over the Bay Street viaduct, the smell of pecan wood cooking ribs on an open pit fire danced in my nose. A dingy barbecue joint was probably not the ideal place to take a woman when you were trying to make a good impression, especially a woman like Ava Lynn Jefferson, but the food was in a class all on its own. I pulled into the gravel parking lot and heard the stones crunching under the tires of my truck. I hadn't seen what car she got into when we ran into each other last, so I wasn't sure which one of the cars in the parking lot belonged to her.

I went inside and glanced around, but I wasn't hit with a ray of sunshine that is her smile, so I knew I had to be the first one there. I was starved, so I went to the counter and ordered. Two things you could expect when you went to that place was shitty service and damn good food. The latter made up for the former.

I got my soda can and sat at one of the tables near the front window. I wanted to be able to see her when she pulled up. The way I was staring out of that dingy little window, you would have thought that I was a man who was possessed, but I was very anxious to see her again. Here I was a married man, acting like I was in puppy love all over again with a woman I hadn't seen in over a decade. I started to question what I was really doing there. What did I think would come of me knowing what had happened with her since I had lost her that first time so many years ago? Did I think that she and I would just pick up where we had left off? I had to get myself under control. It was simply to get the "what ifs" out of my thoughts. If I just had a clear understanding, then this feeling would go away, and I would go back to my life with my family. We would all live happily ever after.

My thoughts must have really taken me off into a trance because a voice saying "Good afternoon, Mr. Sanford" snapped me back into the present. She stood before me with a smile that seemed to brighten up the whole restaurant.

I stood up and went around the table to hug her. "Hi, Ava Lynn. Thank you for meeting me for lunch today. I hope you don't mind. I already ordered food for us because I know their reputation for slow service."

She fit into my arms just as I remembered, and she smelled of expensive perfume. I didn't want to let go, but the time limit had expired for a "friendly hug." See, there were different types of hugs that you give to women. The first is the church hug. This is from the side with limited body contact, so there is no confusion of your intentions. Usually, you do this from the side with one arm, and it lasts about three seconds. Then there is the family hug. This hug is tight and loving, and its length may be extended based on the amount of time that has passed since you last saw the person. This is usually done with an older relative like an aunt, and you hug and rock while saying things, like "It has been so long since I last seen ya" or "Come on over here and give me a hug. I missed you, baby." Then there is the friendly hug used for greeting a woman when you all are out in public or entering each other's company. This is a typical southern hello very similar to a church hug, but you can use both arms, and it lasts about the same amount of time as a church hug. The last hug is the hug you give to a woman when you want to say more than just hello. The length of time that it can last varies and if done right can lead to other things. I did not want to give the impression that this was that last type of hug, but when I saw her smile, I would be lying if I said it did not cross my mind.

"Good, I hope you got ribs and chicken…"

Before she could finish her sentence, I blurted, "…and bread. I remembered that you like to take both meats off the bone, put 'em in the bread together, and dip it in the barbecue sauce to eat it just a little at a time. You used to love strawberry soda, so that is what I got for you. I hope that not too much has changed."

I could see the surprise on her face. She smiled even bigger and asked, "How did you remember all of that? You must have a steel-trap memory." She chuckled, and we immediately fell into an easy conversation.

We ate and talked and talked and talked. Before we knew it, two hours had flown by. She let me know that she talked to her parents, and they confirmed what I had told her happened on my end. She was apologetic about her parents and added that they admitted that they were wrong for their actions. They were simply trying to do what they thought was best for her. Their deception had hurt us both, but we knew there was not anything that could be done to fix old hurts that we had moved past. We just agreed that it was something that happened that no one could take back, and we would leave it at that.

The topic came up that I was most afraid to talk about. *Was I married?* I gave her the full detail of my marriage to Cynthia, my relationship with Donna, and my love for my sons. As I brought her full up to date on what had occurred in my life over the past twelve years, she listened and never seemed to flinch. I thought that by the time I got to the boys, she would have grabbed her purse and said, "Nice to see you again," and darted out the door. Not my Ava. She shared in my joys and seemed to enjoy hearing every detail about me.

Turns out, she had actually gotten married back in sixty-two and had a baby girl who was now four years old. Her husband was called off to Vietnam, and he did not return. Ava Lynn was a widow. After graduating from Paine College, she decided that she wanted to be dentist, so she graduated from Meharry Medical College School of Dentistry and was in Savannah scouting places to set up shop.

She was in line to take over for one of the two black dentists in the city who would be retiring in the next few months. She spent three days a week acclimating herself to the staff and getting to know the patients, and they were getting to know her. She would officially be in the office full time starting in March, and the name on the shingle would change in June when the current doctor officially retired. I could not stop telling her how proud I was of her. She had suffered through some major losses, all while making major accomplishments. I could not help but wonder if the twins had survived would she have graduated from college and went on to complete dental school. This was another one of those times where you just say, "God's will shall be done," and stop trying to figure out the what-ifs.

She asked me a question that shocked me. "I never share this with anyone, but I have a picture of the twins. Would you like to see it? I figure they were your babies, too. If it is too creepy, I understand. No one except my parents has ever seen the photo."

"Yes. I mean, do you have it here with you?"

"No, but my home is not a far drive from here. You could follow me over there if you like."

"Yeah, I would like that." I do not know why I said that. Dead people have always been unsettling to me, and to see my flesh and blood in a photo… I was not sure how I would react. It seemed like it was important to her, so I was willing to oblige.

"Okay, are you familiar with the area called Sylvan Terrace? I live there. It is about a fifteen-minute drive. Just follow me."

We left the Rib Hut and drove over to her house. It was a sunny afternoon, and I was happy to be in her presence. The way that we talked and enjoyed each other's company was smooth like spreading soft butter on a slice of warm bread. I remembered why we had gotten along so good when we were together. It was because we were friends. Glancing out of the window, I could see the scenery change. It went from project housing to beautiful homes. Pulling into her driveway, I knew the home was suited for her. I could tell that the neighborhood was classy before knowing too much about it. Her daughter was in

Augusta with her parents while she was here getting settled. She would move down next summer.

As I walked up the drive to meet her at the back door where she stood, Ava Lynn said, "Welcome to my home. It is not exactly how I want it yet, but it will get there soon."

I went in and sat down at the kitchen table. Everything in this space was modern. There was a green oven, stovetop, and refrigerator lining the walls. The sink was evergreen with silver around the trim. There was linoleum in the kitchen and a shag carpet in the den. It smelled of fresh paint and lemons. It reminded me of what "clean" would smell like if it was an actual scent. There was some artwork on the walls. A big wooden spoon and fork hanging next to each other, and a framed picture of some eggs in a basket. I felt right at home sitting at her table, and I was glad that I didn't have to worry about her husband coming home and shooting me for being in his house. I was sad that she had lost her husband that way in the war, but I had a selfish sigh of relief on the inside knowing that she was no longer married.

She came in with a small stack of pictures in her hand, and she narrated each one. There were pictures of her on her wedding day, which I was glad to rush past. She looked like I imagined she would on her big day but seeing her happy with another man gave me an unsettling feeling in my stomach. Then she shared pictures of her daughter, who was a cute little thing.

Before moving to the last picture in the stack, she asked, "Are you sure want to see them?"

"Yes," I replied to reassure her.

She showed me the picture, and I placed it in my hands and gasped just a little. There were two little faces that looked just like Junior and Kenneth when they were babies. I do not know why, but I started to feel my throat get dry. I coughed a little to clear it away and asked Ava Lynn had she given them names? She then began to give me full details about their births.

"Your daughters, Coretta and Corrine, were born into this world on Thursday, December 6, 1956, at 2:30 pm. Today would have been their twelfth birthday." I looked at her and could see the tears start to run down her cheeks. She wiped at the streams of salty water and sucked in a deep breath. "I know it seems strange that I still get emotional on this date, but I loved them. I wish that I had the chance to be their mom and see them grow. I look at this picture, and it just seems like they are sleeping sweetly."

"Ava Lynn, I am so sorry that I wasn't there for you when they were born. I know there is nothing we can do about the past, but I am glad that you shared this with me today." I leaned over instinctively and kissed her on the forehead, and she fell into my arms weeping. I could tell that she had waited to share this moment with someone else, and I was just happy that I could be here for her.

After Ava Lynn gathered herself, she started making small talk, and I told her how much the girls looked like my two sons when they were born. I asked her if she had gotten a chance to see their eye color, and she told me that they each had eyes like mine. Somehow, I became so overwhelmed talking about my two children that had not breathed in any breath or seen the light of day. I asked where the restroom was, and I just put the picture down so that I could walk out of the kitchen before Ava could see how affected I was. Men do not get this emotional, but I could not help it. I think I was mad again at the Jeffersons for not telling me that Ava Lynn was pregnant. I peed, and while I was shaking dry, I was trying my best to shake this feeling off me. I went back out to the kitchen and sat at the table. I could tell Ava Lynn had been crying again since I left.

"Ava Lynn, I have enjoyed spending time with you today catching up. Thank you so much for sharing the picture with me. I can tell how painful that memory is for you." I grabbed her chin between my thumb and index finger to lift her face up to look at me. The look in her eyes made me want to know what she was thinking. "Ava, baby, tell me what is on your mind."

Ava Lynn stared for a moment and started. "I just knew you would come back into my life. I have never stopped loving you. You are the same as the last time that I saw you, only more muscles now and taller. God! You were my everything back then, Kendall. I lost you behind a lie. Now you are back, and I cannot even have you because you belong to another woman. I can't figure out why I'm being taunted like this."

Her confession shocked me, and before I knew it, I said the same words that I had uttered so many years ago. "Ava, I love you so much. Deep down, I have never stopped loving you."

Before I knew anything, she was on my lap, kissing me while I was pulling her bottom closer to me. I undressed her right there in the kitchen. Her skin was warm and smelled of sweet rosewater. She tasted so sweet as I tried to kiss every inch of her. I knew that Ava Lynn was still mine, and I had to show her in the best way that I knew that I did still love her. She was in tune with me, and I was in tune with her.

That day we made love, and it was just as perfect as the first time that we lost our virginity together on that barn floor so many moons ago. This woman was amazing. We shared something that no one else would be able to say that they shared with us. When we both had finished, we did not talk about where we would go from here. We just held each other and let the moment be.

Chapter 10

"Kenny Boy, what is going on with you lately?" Lester asked while he pretended to punch me in the jaw.

"One of his wives must have been putting it on him real good because this fool been walking around whistling every time that I have seen him for the past two months," added Kevin who was just happy to have someone else to talk about other than himself. He and Lou had been fighting, and she put him out for running around with that new secretary that he had hired for our Savannah office.

My brother, David, asked us to come up to his new house in New York for a brother's weekend, so this is the first time that I had been with all of my brothers at the same time in a couple of years. He couldn't let the other two have all the fun, so he put in his two cents. "Kevin, don't be mad that baby bro got all of his women in check, and he got multiple houses he can go to." They all fell out laughing at that one. I did not laugh, but I knew they were right. Our set up was different.

"Nah, it ain't even like that. Honestly, fellas, I need to get your opinions on something." I got serious, but my older brothers were all still laughing and playing around. They settled down and focused in on me.

"What's on your mind?" David asked.

"Well, I found out recently that I had twin girls." When I glanced up, all three of their jaws had dropped to the floor. I continued, "David, I know you remember the girl that I was in love with in 10th grade. Ava Lynn?" He nodded his head. "Well, I ran into her back in December, and she told me that she had twins that were mine. They didn't make it through birth, but she left me because her parents forced her to go off to boarding school, and I never heard from her again until I bumped into her one day when I had taken Cynt shopping in Savannah." None of my brothers said a word, so I ran down the entire story to them up through that first time that we slept together on the twins' birthday.

"It sounds like you still love this woman, Kenny Boy. Have you seen her again since that day?" Lester questioned. I knew he would be the most skeptical. He did not even wait for me to reply before he asked, "Kenny Boy, is she pregnant for you again?"

"Nah! She ain't pregnant," I said. Though I said that, I would not be surprised if she turned up pregnant one day. It was like we could not get enough of each other. "It's just that we have reconnected, and I am not sure how it's possible, but I still love her."

"So, are you saying you want to leave Cynthia for her?" asked Kevin. "Are you going to leave Donna, too, and move to Savannah and be with her?"

"See, that's the thing! That is just it. I love all three, and I am not going to leave anyone." They all looked puzzled at this point. "I need to know how I can make this work with all of them. Cynthia and Donna know about each other. Ava Lynn knows about both of them, but they do not know about her and what we have going now. I been seeing her for two almost three months, and I don't see us ending it anytime soon."

I knew what I was asking was crazy as hell, but I honestly could not see myself losing Ava Lynn again. Nor could I see me living without Cynthia or Donna in my life. This was a big mess that I had gotten myself into, but I needed some help from the three wise men in my life to help me navigate this situation.

David broke the silence and finally said, "Well, fellas. I think old Kenny Boy has it right. We stopped at one woman, and we are miserable. He has had two women and been open about it for years with no problem. He now wants to add to that. Honestly, if you can make it work, shit, I say go for it."

"If Lou had gone for it, then I wouldn't have been sneaking around doing my dirt. It isn't natural for one man to be with just one woman," Kevin stated. "Now I'm sleeping at the office waiting for my wife to tell me I can come back home to the house that I pay for."

"I'm just fine with my one and only, but to each his own. Kenny Boy, I think if you feel this strongly about it then keep doing what you have always done. Be honest with Cynthia and Donna, and just see what happens. Don't wait until she is pregnant to tell them, though. That might get you straight up killed. I don't feel like shopping for a new suit for your funeral, alright?" said Lester.

Lester did have the perfect wife for him. My love life was set up a little different, though, and I needed to come to terms with that when I got back home.

We left the train station headed into Manhattan to catch the Knicks game at Madison Square Garden. The rest of the weekend was full of beer and bonding with my brothers. No worries about our women. We were just happy that we were together and having good times. David completed the group, and we could all tell that he missed us just as much as we miss him back home.

***

When I got home, things went along as usual on my day-to-day grind. I would see Donna and Cynthia throughout the week, and I would be in Savannah as much as possible. Cynthia and Donna both thought I was in Savannah strictly for work, but mostly it was so I could spend time with Ava.

Being the person that I was, I hated that I could not be honest about my relationship with Ava. I made up my mind that this was it. I had had enough sneaking around. I would tell Cynthia and Donna the truth and see where the dust settled, yet the perfect time never seemed to arrive.

It was the Saturday before Memorial Day, and it was unusually hot for May. Lou had let Kevin come back home, and he had planned this big family holiday weekend for all of us. The kids had talked us into taking them to the beach, so we drove over to Hilton Head Island where some of Lou's friends had a beach house in a section called, Mitchellville, which was mostly owned by affluent black families. I was down on the beach, watching the kids, and having a good time until Kevin came and grabbed me by the shoulder. He pulled me to the side to talk where no one could hear us.

"What is the girl's name that you are seeing here in Savannah? Please tell me her name ain't Dr. Ava Lynn Stevens?"

"Yeah. It is really Jefferson because her husband died. Why are you asking about Ava?"

"Negro, because she is in the house." He looked at me, trying to gauge my reaction. "Kenny Boy, I know how you feel about this girl, and I do not want you to trip out. She is here with someone. He is a lawyer or something."

What! Not my Ava! It just wasn't possible for her to be there with some other man. I mean, I really couldn't be mad if she had gone somewhere with another man, right? Well, either way, I had to see if this was my Ava for myself. I almost broke into a sprint from the beach up towards the house. I had to gain my composure, though because I could not let my family (especially Cynthia) know that something was up.

I walked into the kitchen, and there she was. She had not seen me yet, but I could definitely see all of her. She had on a white bikini with one of those long cover-ups that the women wear. She could not hide those hips. I knew them anywhere. After lurking for a few minutes, I went into the kitchen where she was talking to my sister-in-law. They had just met, and they were making small talk. When Lou spotted me, she called me over.

"Kenny Boy, I want you to meet some people. This is Mr. Brian Robinson. He is visiting from Augusta, where he practices law." Brian reached over to shake my hand, and the whole time, I did not take my eyes off Ava Lynn.

"How are you doing? I am Kendall Sanford. My family is in town for the holiday weekend from Darien." I was still looking at Ava Lynn waiting for an introduction.

He turned to Ava Lynn, "Hey, didn't you guys live in Darien before moving to Augusta?"

"Yes, we sure did." She smiled at him as she said it. "I know Kendall from high school. We go way back. Tenth grade, right?" she asked me. I could not believe it. She was getting a kick out of it. She could tell I was jealous, but since I was married, there was not a thing that I could do about it.

"Ralph Bunche High School. Those were some of the best days of my life." I just continued with my intense look.

Brian turned to Ava Lynn, "See you do know someone here." He laughed and then turned to talk to Lou and I. "You see my cousin wanted to stay in the house and sit by the phone waiting for this mystery man to call her. I told her that while I was in town, she was going to do more than just sit up in the house looking at the four walls."

She rolled her eyes at him and waved him off as he went out of the patio door and headed towards the water.

He said cousin. She was not with some man. She was with a relative. My entire demeanor relaxed. Lou had got bored of the whole

74

scene since she was not the center of attention, and she trotted out to the beach right behind Brian.

Realizing we were alone in the kitchen, she turned to me with a very serious look on her face.

"Is your wife here? You said your family was in town. Do you mean to tell me I have to look at Cynthia? Or is Donna with you? And pretend that we are not in love?" Her eyebrows started to pinch together at the top of her nose. I could tell she was about to get real pissed.

"Yes, Cynthia is here. Both of my sons are here, too." I was not as nervous as I probably should have been, but for some reason, a strange calm had come over me.

"Kendall, why are you acting like this is no big deal?"

"Because it's not. I love you, Ava Baby, and one day you were going to have to meet everyone anyway. Looks like God is forcing it to happen today." I just smiled, and for some reason, I knew things would work out whatever that might look like it was going to be whatever it was.

I took her hand into mine and walked out to the beach towards my family. I introduced her to my brothers and their wives and reintroduced her to Cynthia. She had remembered her from when we were younger. Cynthia noticed that I was touching her a lot, but I knew Cynthia. She would not make a scene even if she had suspected something. We all ended up having a great time splashing around in the water and watching the kids play. When we laid out in the sand, Cynthia was to the right, and Ava was on my left side of me. Neither was neglected, and I made sure to pay special attention to both when we were alone for brief moments. Around five, we were getting ready to go up to the house to eat barbecue, and I found myself alone with Cynthia. She decided it was a good time to talk.

"So, Kenny, how long has she been back in your life?" Cynthia quizzed.

"For about the past six months. Cynthia, I promise I wanted to tell you about us, but I just did not know how. You are already accepting of Donna, but I wasn't sure how you would feel about another woman."

We both stood still facing each other at this point. I decided to break the silence.

"Cynthia, you know I love you, and I always will. You also know that I love Donna, and Ava Lynn was the first love that I ever had." I probably should have stopped there, but my mind would not let me. "You are my wife, and I promised to always take care of you. Nothing will ever make me break that promise."

"Kendall, I knew who you were when I married you. You are a good man, and you love very hard. I knew something was different, but I didn't know that the something different was another woman that I was going to have to start sharing you with." Her eyes started to well up with tears, but she quickly wiped them away. "Kenny, I love you, too, baby. Despite the way things look on the outside, you always make sure I am happy. My son, no wait. Our sons never want for anything. What more can I ask for from a man that has a penchant for loving multiple women all at the same time?"

I was shocked that she truly got me. There was no big blow up or hassle. She just went along with it.

Ava Lynn came walking up the path where we were. Cynthia started, "Ava Lynn, Kendall shared everything about you guys' relationship with me. I know that he loves you and I can tell that you are in love with him as well. I just want you to know that I understand, and as long as you understand that I am his wife first, we will not have any problems."

I could tell that Ava Lynn was stunned because all she said to that was, "Okay." I told her that everything was going to be fine.

***

76

Things were fine until I told Donna about finding Ava Lynn and explained that she was now going to be a part of my life. Her reaction was the polar opposite of Cynt's. She walked around the house and cursed for what seemed like forever. I sat for a while and listened, hoping for a break in her ranting. No such luck. Finally, I just had to cut her off when she started packing bags.

"Donna, where are you going?" I asked with a little more bass in my voice. I was growing irritated at the thought of her actually leaving me.

"Look, I can't do this no more. I was a fool to stick around even though I know you are married to Cynthia. I would be fucking crazy to not get out of this...this...shit! What the hell is this that we are doing? We don't even know. I am an educated woman, and I can take care of Kenneth and me. I don't need this shit." She slammed more clothes in the bag.

"So, you are just going to up and leave with my son? Don't you think I have a say so in where you take my child? He is mine, too." I wanted to say something else, but I learned my lesson about that when she first told me that she was pregnant. Plus, I knew that he was mine, so there was no need to throw water on a grease fire.

"Look, Kendall. This is the deal. I deserve to be the apple of my man's eye. I deserve to be his one and only lover. I deserve to have a husband, too. This is not going to work for me anymore. I know that you have been honest with me. You have been good to me, and you love your son. The only person that has not been honest with me is me." She laughed under her breath, then continued, "I have to be honest with myself. This arrangement is never going to completely make me happy. This is not what I want for my life, and if I stay here, I will never truly be happy."

She got me with the marriage thing. I had never thought about the fact that maybe she wanted someone who could marry her. We sat in silence for a few moments then I spoke.

"Donna, you do know that I love you, right? Why does it matter that we don't have a piece of paper to proclaim that you are my wife?" I had to keep calm because I could feel resentment start to surface. I took a deep breath in and started slowly, "Donna, please tell me what things other than the piece of paper are you looking for in a marriage that I don't already give you."

"How about coming home to me every night?" She replied too quickly, so I knew she had already thought this out. She did not stop there. "What about being able to have the same last name as my child? What about me not having people talk about me as a second rate person in your life? Kendall, these are all things that you don't see. Sure, you pay bills and help me raise our son, but what about the little things?" Her voice quivered a little then she started up again. "Where were you on Christmas Day, huh? While you were with your wife at the big family dinner, I had to sit here and wait for you all alone like some insignificant piece of nothing. That is the part you are missing, Kendall." She stopped packing, and I could see clarity wash over her like waves crashing into the shore. She moved next to me, grabbed my shoulders, and turned me towards her. "Kendall, I love you, but I… AM…DONE."

After she said that last part, she did not say another word to me no matter what I said or how much I begged and pleaded for her not to leave. I surrendered to the fact that this was just the straw that broke the camel's back. She apparently had these feelings tucked away for a while but announcing that Ava Lynn and I had rekindled a flame that blew out so long ago pushed her beyond her limits.

Donna let Kenneth stay with me for the summer because the boys would be working with their uncles and me. I also knew that it would be easier for her to get settled if he was out of her hair. She was a fiery woman, and her speech was believable. However, I knew she was not completely over me. She would tell me to meet her at the "old house" and not bring the boys so we could talk and get some "closure." Really, we never talked about much. There was more body-to-body contact than anything else happening. This happened at least once a week, and I cannot say that I minded one bit. I still loved her, and we never had any problems in the bedroom. I just could not give her what she wanted in terms of being the only woman in my life.

Donna's transition happened at a good time for her because she had been offered a new position as the Assistant Chief of Nursing at Brunswick Regional Hospital, breaking another barrier and adding another "first Negro to do this" to her resume. She found a nice house in town that was not far from the hospital. I was glad that she was not too far away, so I could still see Kenneth as much as I wanted to. She originally talked about moving to Atlanta, but I think the reality that she would be so far away from everything that she loved cleared that notion from her brain.

I tried to get her to let Kenneth live with Cynthia and me so that he did not have to go to a new school, but she was not going for it. Instead, I would pick him up every Friday, and he would be in Darien, or Junior would go to Brunswick with them so the boys would at least be together. I am glad that she and Cynthia both cared for each other's son as if he were their own. I knew many guys who couldn't bring their kids around the new wife or girlfriend, but I think that speaks to that woman's character as well as her heart. Women are nurturers by nature, and I used my mother as an example. Janie came in this world by way of an extramarital affair, yet Mama loved her as her own because she was a part of my father, the man that Mama loved unconditionally until the day he died.

Chapter 11

Marvin Gaye was singing *Heard it Through the Grapevine* over the radio as I drove along I-95 headed to Savannah for my weekly visits. We had canceled our business meeting this week because Lester was taking Bell to a baby doctor's appointment. She had three miscarriages over the past two years, and this time, they were taking every precaution. I could tell that the miscarriages were taking a toll on them both. They wanted to grow their family (meaning Lester really wanted a son) and wanted to make sure they were doing everything right this time around. Any time that Bell looked like she gained a little weight, we would all give each other a knowing look. Since we all knew it was a sensitive subject, we all would hang back and wait for one of them to tell us any news, be it positive or negative.

Driving into Savannah was one of the highlights of my week. There was something about the old buildings and the feel of the city. Even if you were smacked with a funky odor when you crossed the city limits, that meant good business for my brothers and me, so I would gladly sniff it any day. My first stop was to Ava's house. I picked her up, and we headed over to Larry's for breakfast. The breakfast at Larry's was the best in the city, so we did not mind going there instead of eating at home.

"Kendall, I have a few patients to see this morning. I promised that I would take them because they are having dental emergencies. I hope you don't mind," Ava Lynn said as we finished breakfast.

"No problem. I will take care of some business while I wait for you to get done. I thought we might catch that new movie, *Shaft*. What time do you think you will finish up?"

"Not sure, but hopefully I will be done no later than one o'clock," she said with the biggest smile on her face.

"Ava, why you sitting over there grinning like a catfish?" She is usually happy when we are together, but this smile was different today.

"Well, what if I told you that I love you, and I am glad that we found each other again?" She was looking as if something was tickling her.

"Yes, we found each other over two years ago, and things could not be better," I stated because the truth was things were great. The business was doing better than ever. I even ventured out into some other side hustles that were stacking money to pay for my boys' and Sandra's, Ava's daughter, college tuition.

"So, what if I told you that I think history was about to repeat itself?" She stared at me, awaiting my response.

Honestly, this confused me. I was not real sure what she was talking about. "Ava Lynn, woman, what are you talking about?"

"Kendall, how do I look to you? Does anything look different at all?"

Then the lightbulb went off. I sat shocked and stared at her real good. I knew she had picked up a few pounds, but there was no way that she could be pregnant. I knew I had better choose my words carefully, so I was slow to speak.

"You are the same beautiful woman that I fell in love with at the age of fifteen. Not much has changed on you other than you get prettier every time that I see that smile of yours." Ava Lynn knew that I was bullshitting her because I could see the bridge of her nose tighten up.

"Well, Kendall Sanford, according to my doctor, you are going to have another baby." She was smiling so hard she did not even wait for me to say anything. Before I knew it, she was on my side of the table hugging and kissing me.

"WOW! Wait. How long have you known?"

"I thought something was different last month, but I went to the doctor, and sure enough, we are having a baby next December." She squealed that last part out. I guess this response was because of our age and where we were in our lives.

The first time I got a girl pregnant, I did not know, and her parents ran off and hid it from me. The next two times, I was forced to get married to one of the girls, and the other was mad at me for not marrying her. This time it seemed like I was free to be happy about the baby, and it did not feel like I was in the middle of a crisis. I was not sure what to do to express how I was feeling at that moment, because honestly, I was numb.

What I did was get my excitement level up to match hers. I kissed her on the forehead and said, "This is great news, baby!"

I wondered what her parents would say this time around. It did not really matter because this time they were not getting rid of me or stashing away my girl. I was a man, and I was able to take care of Ava Lynn and our baby. OUR BABY. God really had a funny way of answering your prayers. When I used to pray that Ava Lynn would come back and for us to have a second chance, I would have never guessed that I would be here all these years later with the love of my life celebrating her pregnancy.

***

During the entire pregnancy, Ava Lynn was sure that she felt different from when she had Sandra. Her feet were swollen, and things were bulging in places that I had never imagined that a woman would bulge. The closest description that I could give of her body would be two basketballs under her shirt. Her nose looked as if the edges of her nostrils reached the corners of her mouth. It had gotten so wide. As bad as it was on her, I still thought she was attractive. Hell, I found my way into her bed more then than ever before, probably. The white lady on TV, Dr. Ruth, said that having sex during pregnancy would help the mama's back pain, and the closer you got to the due date, it might make the baby come on out. Whatever she said meant something to Ava Lynn, but not me. I was just horny, and for some reason, she was turning me on, so that made for a great match.

Cynthia had resigned to the fact that I should be with Ava Lynn when the baby came, so she did not put up much of an argument when I began spending more time in Savannah. I would check in regularly, but I was spending more nights in Savannah.

Ava Lynn worked at her practice until she went into labor. She was mid-check-up on a patient when her water broke. Lucky for us, her cover doctor, a recent Meharry dental graduate, was already learning the office. She was able to step in, and the office did not have to shut down. Everyone could still be paid.

The day that her water broke was ironically on December 6, 1971 (fifteen years to the day that our first set of twins were born) and the birth was very quick. The doctor said she almost didn't make it to the hospital.

I saw the doctor walking out in the hallway to look for me. "Hey Doc, what's the news on Ava Lynn?"

"She is doing just fine. This was one of the easiest births that I have seen with multiple births. She just spit those babies out like it wasn't nothing," he said. "Congratulations! You got yourself a pair of girls."

"Wait, did you say two girls? So, she had twins?"

"Yeah, there were two babies. Surprised us all," the doctor said with a big grin on his face. "You ready to go see her and your brand new baby girls?"

I nodded, shook his hand, and went into the room where Ava Lynn was. I had gone by the gift shop and gotten a big bunch of flowers. When I walked into the room with them, Ava lit up even more.

"Oh, Kendall, we have twin girls." Just then, another nurse came in to check on her. They poked, prodded, checked then rechecked everything on her what seemed like every few minutes. When the thermometer was out of her mouth, she asked, "Did you go down to the nursery and see them yet?"

The nurse chimed in. "Wait a few minutes, and I will bring them in for you. You should try to nurse them if you are thinking about breastfeeding. Although, for two babies, most mothers use formula, and I don't see how it would be possible to nurse two babies at once. I will bring the babies in, and you let me know when I get back with them. I will help you with whatever way you want to feed those beauties." Then off she went without Ava Lynn getting a word in.

"I guess you are about to meet your daughters," she said, still smiling. Even though the way that the nurse spoke would have sent Donna off the deep end, Ava Lynn was so happy nothing could have upset her.

"So, are you going to nurse or bottle-feed them? I think you need to have an answer for that nurse when she gets back. She seems to run a really tight ship." I did not care, either way, I just want to make sure they were fed.

"I used formula with Sandra, so these two will probably get formula, too," she said.

I was not sure what I was expecting to see when they brought the babies in, but one was brown like Ava with blue eyes, and one was light with greyish green eyes. The light one looked exactly like Junior and Kenneth when they were babies. She said the darker one looked like Sandra when she was a baby, minus the eye color.

The nurse who was an older black woman decided to speak her

peace again without any prompting. "Don't get too fixed on them babies staying that light or keeping them light eyes. Look at their ears and fingernail beds. That will be the tell-tale sign." She inspected them both and handed one to Ava Lynn and one to me. "I suspect since you so fair they might actually stay a little light but don't count on it."

"Both of my girls are beautiful, and their complexion doesn't really matter none to us. We have healthy babies, and their mama is fine. What more could we ask for?" I said dismissing all of her talk of skin color. I know some black folks feel a certain way when it comes to being fair-skinned, and then there is that business of passing brown paper bag tests. However, that was all pure bullshit in my mind. In this world that we live in, no matter what, someone somewhere will look at you, and all they will see is a nigger. My daddy taught me that, and he also taught me how to deal with the world and how not to allow the ignorance of others to keep me from being great. I felt it was my duty to teach all of my kids the same lessons that I was taught by my daddy.

I guess the nurse sensed that I was getting aggravated, and she decided to hold her mule. She moved quickly to get formula to feed the babies. Then she made herself scarce the rest of the time Ava Lynn was under her care.

"So, what are you going to name them?" I asked Ava, hoping that it was something that started with a K. She knew how I felt about it because we often joked about it.

"I already had planned on the name Kenley if it was a girl. Now that we have two girls, I suppose I need to think of another name."

"What about Kimberly," I suggested.

"I think I like that. Kenley and Kimberly Sanford, you have names," she said as she caressed one babies head that was lying on her lap and kissed the forehead of the one that she was nursing.

Looking at Ava Lynn with the babies like that on the hospital bed made me start to drift off into what-ifs. What if the twins she gave birth to when we were teenagers had lived? What if her parents had told me the truth, and not kept the pregnancy a secret from me? What if we had been allowed to be together as a family so long ago? So many what-if's, but life is like that sometimes. You just never know how things would have turned out if certain things had or had not happened. All you can do is live in the right now and make the best of the life that you were given.

I left the hospital and headed back to Ava Lynn's house after she had dinner, and the nurses took the babies back to the nursery. I called my wife to let her know that the babies had been born. She was so funny. She never spoke of Ava Lynn and did not want me to speak of her in her presence. However, since she found out that Ava Lynn was pregnant, she was all of a sudden consumed with knowing how Ava was doing. I swear this woman was funny as hell, but I knew that she was gonna love the girls just like she loved Kenneth. She asked the typical questions and was shocked that I had twins.

After I hung up the phone from Cynthia, I walked around the house for a little while. I got an unsettled feeling and decided to drive to Darien. Without Ava being there, I did not feel right being in the house. I had to be at work in the morning anyway, so it made sense for me to go home to be near the office. Ava Lynn's doctor told me to come back tomorrow at 4:30 because I should have been able to take Ava Lynn and the babies home the next evening.

***

"Big brother, I heard you made me an auntie again," Janie sang as I walked into the office. I hated that she was around so many men, but she was fresh out of college and served as the office manager for all three of our locations. She traveled between the offices to pay all of the bills, keep tabs on all of the clerical work, and started learning the business.

"I see Mama couldn't keep the good news to herself." I kissed her on the cheek and headed into my private office.

"How exciting! Twin girls. I cannot wait to meet them. When do you think I can see them? I bet they are beauties."

"Actually, one of them looks just like you did when you were a baby. I think it's the eyes. I see you, Junior, and Kenneth as babies when I look at them. These Sanford genes are strong," I said as I started flipping through the invoices for the truck yard.

Damn, we are paying more in payroll again. We need to add that to our weekly meetings so that we stay in front of it, I thought to myself. "I am going to Savannah tonight. If you want to ride with me, you can tag along and help us take the babies home. I've got a feeling that we are going to need some extra hands."

"Yes, that works perfectly. I have to go to the Savannah office tomorrow so I can stay with my friend tonight, and go into work tomorrow," Janie said with extra excitement.

It hit me at about lunchtime that Ava Lynn only had one of everything at her house. There wasn't anywhere for the second baby to sleep. I told Janie that she and I would wrap up early and then head to Savannah. We went to the baby furniture store and picked up another bassinette to match the one that was already purchased. We also bought some sheets and other items that Janie talked me into believing Ava Lynn definitely needed for the baby. After we dropped all of our purchases off at the house, we made it to the hospital just as the doctor was headed to Ava Lynn's room.

"Mr. Sanford, I was just about to release Ava Lynn to go home. She was doing well today, and should be ready to go," the doctor told us. He looked at Janie with a curious eye. I could not tell if he thought that she was pretty and was interested or if he thought we were together. I know that Ava Lynn shared that I had a wife, which was why she and I were not married. Did he think that Janie was Cynthia?

I pointed towards Janie. "Excuse this country boy. Where are my manners? Doc, this is my baby sister, Janie Sanford. Janie, this is Ava's doctor, Theophilus Stevens."

"Pleasure to meet you, Miss Sanford. Congratulations on the birth of your two beautiful nieces," he aimed at her. Now it was clear. Another dude who thought my sister was cute.

After standing there in the hallway with those two for a few moments, it was obvious that I was quickly becoming a third wheel. I decided to leave them two alone to talk and went into the room with Ava Lynn. She was sitting up on the bed. The nurse had the babies all bundled and ready to be taken home.

"I hope you don't mind. I brought back up to help get the twins home," I said as I kissed Ava Lynn. "You think you are ready to make this trip home?"

"I am as ready as I am ever going to be, Mr. Sanford." She turned to the nurse. "It is time for me to stop being spoiled and go home and be a mommy."

The nurse loaded Ava up in the wheelchair, then placed the babies in each of her arms, and we were off to tackle this new life with twin girls. Her mother was due to arrive tonight and help with the girls.

Chapter 12

Smoke was coming out of my mouth as I yelled hello across the parking lot to some of my friends that I saw as I was leaving the football game. Every Friday during the fall, everyone in town would go to the football game and then head off to their respective after-game hangouts. My place of choice these days was to hang out over at the Shady Oak, which was a juke joint way back in the woods. It sat in the middle of an old community called Sandtown, which you would never be able to locate on a map. But everyone from around the area knew exactly where it was. It was a wooden shack with a big tree painted on the front of it. The club got its name because of all of the Great Oak trees on the property. Mr. Lee, the owner of the club, lived right next door in his trailer. His wife was a sweet church-going woman named Emmie, who would never be caught in that club of her husband's.

Though it was well known that any woman brave enough to try to chase after Mr. Lee would come to a day of reckoning. That sweet churchwoman could fight like nobody's business, and was not afraid to light someone up who thought they could have a chance at stealing old Lee out from under her. One lady used to come every weekend and whisper in Mr. Lee's ear, telling him all the dirty things that she would do to him if she had the chance. Well somehow, Emmie found out and showed up next door to the club right at the time that the woman showed up. Let's just say that she nor any other woman tried to go after Lee again for fear of having to deal with his crazy wife. She did not beat this lady or nothing like that. What happened was she gave the woman a warning that Lee was a married man, and told her to stay away from him.

Evidently, this woman didn't understand the level of crazy that she was up against, and the woman got flip at the mouth. She said she was a grown-ass woman, and if she wanted to come and talk to Lee, she damn well would. Emmie being the nice churchwoman that she was said a resounding "Okay" and quietly left out of the club. That was not the end of it, though. That lady that was trying her best to screw Mr. Lee. Her house mysteriously burned down that same night. We all knew it was Emmie that did it, but the police could not prove it. When anyone ever brought it up to Emmie, trying to tell her it was not right to burn that lady's house down, her reply was always the same. "God don't like ugly and he ain't too fond of cute either. I didn't do it, but if she wasn't such a hoe then maybe she wouldn't have found herself living out in the streets. Then again, a hoe belong on the street so she right where she belongs." She never did admit to it, but everyone in town knew what time it was.

I liked going to the Shady Oak because I could unwind. Sometimes life would get too heavy between Cynthia, Ava Lynn, and all the kids. I just needed a space to get my mind right. When you were there, you could have whatever was your pleasure. Whatever was your poison, you could find it at the Shady Oak. Reefer was my drug of choice until I got introduced to the white pony. I was one of the few people in town that could actually afford to buy it, and because of that, I usually found myself with quite a few friends when I was getting high. I usually only indulged on the weekends, but that indulgence soon turned into a habit. I was stopping by the Shady Oak more than occasionally. Then I decided that I would just get enough to last me throughout the week. I would keep my stash at the office, and snort whenever I would get the urge. I came home soaring like a kite one too many times, and Cynthia put my ass out. Which really was no biggie to me because I just went up the road to my other place, Donna's old house. I did not even have to worry about getting no monkey. What Cynthia would not give me I got from one of the gals at the Shady Oak. They would gladly come home with me if they knew they were going to get some free blow.

As much as I snorted when I was in Darien, I would never get high if I had to go to Savannah around my girls. It was something about them and their mama that made me want to make sure they never saw that side of me. One night after work, I decided that I wanted to see Kenneth and Donna. I called Donna and asked what she was cooking for dinner. Also, I wanted to know if it was alright if I came by to see Kenneth. She told me that it was cube steak, and of course, it was okay if I came over. I drove down, and my mind was clear. When I pulled into the driveway, I unfolded a little tin foil stash that I had in my wallet. I scooped a little on my pinky, sniffed it up, then wiped the last little residue onto my teeth. Walking up to the door, I felt like Superman.

Donna opened the door, and she was still in her white nurse's uniform. For some reason, she really was looking fine. I pulled her in to kiss her hard on the mouth, and then I started grabbing handfuls of ass, while still standing in the doorway. She pushed me away and told me to stop playing so much. We went into the house, ate dinner, and all was just fine. I was not as high as I wanted to be, so I went to the bathroom and took another hit. That took me where I wanted to be. Now I just wanted Donna to be good to me. I made my way out of the bathroom into the kitchen where Donna was. The instant that I saw her, I decided right then that I needed to feel her and would not take no for an answer. At first, she did not seem to mind me kissing on her neck. She just playfully pushed me off and told me that I lost those privileges long ago. I knew she did not mean that. In my mind, I knew she wanted me just as bad as I wanted her. The more I tried, the more she said no.

"Kendall, have you lost your mind!" Donna shouted at me, hoping to get through to me.

"Come on, Donna. You know you want it, and I shole want you. Stop playing and give me what's mine, girl." I started grabbing her a little harder, trying to push her into the bedroom.

"Kendall Sanford, are you high?"

"No, baby. I just want to get a taste. Come on now and give me some of that monkey," I said, still grabbing at her. I could feel her pushing my hands as hard as she could, trying to get me away from her.

"Kendall, I think it is time for you to go. LEAVE!" Donna was getting angrier by the minute. The more she fought me, the more turned on I got.

After a few more minutes of tussling and trying to get her to give in to me, I felt a hollowness in my stomach, and I immediately dropped to my knees. I grabbed at my balls, but I could not make a sound. My breath had been kicked out of me, literally.

"Bitch! You are going to pay for that!" I hurled at her as I finally got myself together. I felt a rage inside of me that I had never felt before. It was similar to what I imagined Dr. David Banner must have felt as he morphed into the Hulk. I got up from the floor and lunged at Donna, punching her in the right shoulder. I was aiming for her head, but I guess my balance was not quite back yet. Then I grabbed her by the arm to steady myself and slapped her across the face. She flew across the room like a rag doll. No time passed before I was right there on top of her, kicking her on the floor. She tried to stand up, and I pushed her back down. Then out of nowhere, I heard a ringing sound in my right ear. I turned around to see Kenneth standing in the doorway with a pistol in his hand. He had shot so close to my head I could smell the gunpowder.

"Leave my Mama alone," Kenneth stated without any emotion on his face. He just stood in the doorway, holding the gun still aimed with his sight set on me. My own son was willing to kill me. *What the fuck is going on here?*

"Kenneth, sweetie, everything is all right. Put, put the gun down, son," Donna pleaded with him from the floor. After she saw that I was not moving, Donna got up and moved towards Kenneth to get the gun. He never once wavered, but when she reached him, he did give it to his mother.

I got mad all over again and started in on Kenneth. "You ungrateful little bastard. How dare you shoot at me? You think you a man, huh? Then fight me like a motherfucking man, since you thank you a motherfucking man!"

Just as I went to land a punch on my second oldest son, I blanked out, and everything went dark.

***

I blinked once, and I saw a bright white light against the off-white ceiling tiles. I opened my eyes again for a brief moment, and I saw people in blue caps. Heaven had angels, not people in blue caps and blue shirts, so I knew I wasn't dead. I fluttered my eyes open again. I saw lots of people moving around me, but no one was talking to me. I closed my eyes again and took a little nap.

I heard my brother's voice, but I was not very sure at first which one it was. He was saying, "This is what happens when you play with people's emotions. I told this nigga he was gonna get shot one day."

I spoke without opening my eyes. "Who got shot? What y'all talking about?"

"Kenny Boy, can you hear me? It's me, David," my brother said.

"David? David, what are you doing here? Wait, where am I?" I asked as I finally opened my eyes to see my brother, mother, and Cynthia sitting in the room waiting for me to open my eyes.

"Kendall, you been unconscious for the past day. You are in the hospital, son," my mama said in a soothing voice. I could tell that she was nervous but happy that she was able to talk to me. She kept talking. "Kendall, do you remember anything? Can you tell us anything about what happened, baby?"

I looked around the room, and I met eyes with Cynthia. I smiled, and she smiled back at me. I started to scoot like I was trying to sit up, and a nurse who had come in the room to take my vitals pushed a button that made the bed push me into a seated position.

"Cynthia, we need one of these at home, don't we?" Everyone in the room laughed and let out a sigh of relief all in the same breath. I looked at my mother, and I tried to answer her question.

"No, I don't remember what happened." My thoughts were fuzzy, and I could not recollect right off what made me end up in this hospital bed.

"Whatever happened, it sure is making my leg hurt." I started to feel the pain in my thigh.

"Kenny Boy, you really don't remember getting shot?" questioned David.

"What? Tell me what happened. Maybe it will come back to me." I was bothered that I could not remember, but I did not want them to see that.

The door to the hospital room opened and in walked an older white man in a long white coat who I assumed was the doctor.

"Good afternoon, everyone. I am Dr. Mathis. Do you mind if I talk to Mr. Sanford for a few moments?" He gestured for everyone to leave the room. Everyone got up to leave except Cynthia. She told the doctor she was my wife and that she was staying so that she could know what was going on with her husband. He agreed and began talking to me.

"Mr. Sanford, I am glad to see that you are awake. How are you feeling? Is there any pain in that leg?"

"Yes. I was just saying to my family that my leg was hurting pretty bad. Doc, I really don't remember what happened, and I don't remember getting shot."

"Well, Mr. Sanford, that is what I wanted to talk to you about. It is a miracle that you are still here with us. Your blood work came back, showing that you were pretty loaded on cocaine. We ran a toxicology report just to be certain of what we were dealing with, and the levels that were in your system are what we usually see in our OD cases. Mr. Sanford, being shot might have saved your life."

I could see Cynthia start to tear up behind the doctor. She kept quiet, but I know it was killing her not to say something.

"Mr. Sanford, I am recommending that you be checked into the Jacksonville Rehabilitation Unit until you are clean. They have physical therapy along with a drug rehab unit, so it can be a discreet process for you. No one will need to know that you are there for drug rehab."

I did not know what to say. All I could get out was, "Doc, I ain't no junkie. I get high sometimes for fun, but that don't mean I can't quit on my own. I don't need no got damn drug rehab."

Cynthia couldn't take it anymore. She had to break her silence. "So, me putting you out of the house wasn't enough? Donna damn near shooting your dick off wasn't enough? Kendall, when are you going to realize you have a problem?" Cynthia was in full-blown meltdown mode now. "Kendall, we all love you, but you have to see that not only is this drug habit of yours hurting you, but you are also hurting the very people that you claim you love. Kendall, please for the love of God, don't be such a stubborn ass on this. Go to the rehab!"

The doctor turned bright red the moment she mentioned Donna shooting me. I could tell that he was uncomfortable now, but he was too professional to let that stop him from having the conversation that needed to be had. I looked back and forth between the doctor and Cynthia before I finally spoke. "Well, Doc, looks like I will be in rehab for this leg and for my love of cocaine."

"Very good! We will keep you here for a few more days to make sure that you are stable, and then we will get you set up at the rehab facility," Dr. Mathis told me. He shook my hand and then left.

"Cynthia, you said that Donna shot me?" I asked her after the doctor left. "Why did she shoot me?"

She recounted to me what had happened. Donna had two fractured ribs and some bruises, but she was at home resting and would be fine. She did not press charges against me, which is the only reason that I was not handcuffed to the hospital bed.

How could I have done that to Donna? Who was I? This was not what a real man did. My father probably turned over in his grave. I was sad and ashamed. I had to let her know that this was a mistake and that I would never hurt her. *Oh, God, what did I do?*

"Cynthia, I'm sorry. This is not me." I shared my feelings with my wife.

"I'm not the one that you should be apologizing to. Her name is Donna, and you should know that she does have a restraining order out against you, so I hope you don't get it in your head to try and up and go see her," Cynthia told me with a calm tone. She was a little too calm.

"Cynthia, where is Kenneth? Does he know about this?"

"Actually, Kendall, Kenneth was going to shoot you first, but he missed. You see this is why I wouldn't allow you to come into our home. I could see this thing coming five miles away. Once them drugs get a holt to ya, people morph into unrecognizable beings. Kendall, you let this creep up into your spirit, and this demon has taken over. When you start to hurt the people you love, you got to know that it just ain't worth it." Cynthia paused and walked over to the window to look out at the river. "This could have easily been me sitting up at home with a busted up body and a son that was ready to commit murder to protect me."

The door swung open again, and it was my brother and my mother returning. This time they had Janie Mae with them. Janie Mae walked over to the bed and hugged me with all she had and started crying.

"When I found out that you had been shot, I thought you were dead. I am so glad you are alright," she said through her tears.

"I'm fine, Janie. I am going to be just fine. Don't cry, little sister, I am fine," I told her trying to comfort her.

When she settled down, I felt moved in my spirit to say something to everyone. "I am so glad that you all are here with me. I need to get something off my chest and now is just as good a time as any. I honestly had no idea that I had been shot or who shot me until Cynthia just told me what happened."

"Son, you need to rest. Don't get yourself worked up," my mama said, trying to make sure I remained relaxed during recovery.

"I know, Mama, but I have to say this. If I can say it aloud, then that makes me accountable. You see for the past few years I have been doing drugs. Well, I have been on cocaine, and I have let my life spiral out of control. I thought that I was just doing it for fun, but now I find myself doing it all the time." I did not stop talking even though I could tell my mother was visibly upset. I had to finish.

"When y'all left out, the doctor told me that I had enough cocaine in my system when I came in here to have actually overdosed. I am not ready to die. I have a lot to live for. All of you, my family. So, the doctor is putting me in rehab when I leave this hospital. My promise to you today is that I will get this thing off of me, and I will not hurt my family the way that I have been lately. For Kenneth," I started to choke on my words. "For my own son to try and kill me. I ain't right, and I gotta get right before I lose everyone that I love."

I took a deep breath in and blew it out slowly. Cynthia and my mother each came to the bed and hugged me tightly. I knew that I was still surrounded by people who loved me in spite of myself. Now I had to go and make things right with Kenneth and Donna.

***

The first thing I learned in rehab was that getting off this drug was not as easy as I thought it would be. From what they told me, usually cocaine addicts come off the drug easy. I guess I had done so much for so long that I was not the normal patient. I would feel cold, but I would be sweating at the same time. Then I couldn't get my feet to stop shaking, which prolonged my leg rehab. Then I would have pain everywhere in my body, especially in my leg. The therapists and doctors couldn't tell if the pain in my leg was from nerve damage from the gunshot wound or the drug abuse. Either way, I was a mess. I stayed in that rehab facility for a little over a month before they let me go home. They gave me some medicine to curb the cravings that I had to get high. Cynthia had put me out of the house because she knew I was on drugs, but now that I had been through rehab, she let me come back home. I think that was mostly so she could keep an eye on me and make sure I was doing the right things.

During my time in the hospital and rehab, I had not seen the twins. Ava Lynn came down to see me a few times, but I told her I did not want the girls to know anything about it or to see me laid up like I was. I had not heard anything from Donna or Kenneth that entire time. After checking in on the restraining order that Donna had out on me, I found out it had expired, so I felt it was time that I call her.

The phone rang three times, and on the fourth ring, someone finally answered. "Hello?"

"Hello, is Donna home?" I asked, feeling annoyed that it wasn't her that answered.

"She is not home right now. Can I take a message," asked the unknown person.

"This is Kendall. Is Kenneth there?"

"No, he isn't here, either. I will tell her that you called." CLICK! Whoever that was must have known what I had done, because he was not pleased at all that I had called looking for Donna. I would try again later, and if I could not reach her at home, I would catch her at the hospital.

I went on about my day. I tried to reach them a few more times with no luck. I had to figure out where Kenneth and Donna were. If anyone knew their whereabouts for sure, it would be Junior.

"Junior!" I hollered down the hall towards his bedroom. He came up to the front of the house and entered the den where I was sitting. At seventeen, Junior was tall enough to look me in the eye, and he was muscular from playing sports.

"What's up, Pops?"

"Have you talked to your brother? I haven't been able to reach him or Donna on the phone, and I figured you would know where they are."

"Nah! I ain't seen Kenneth in a few days. I know he was talking about some new dude his mom was dating, and that he really liked him."

Well, that answered the question about who was answering the phone at her house.

"Junior, what are you and Kenneth planning to do over the break? I know you all have something cooked up?"

"Nah, I got that basketball tournament, and then I am hanging around for practice. Plus, Samantha's family invited me over for their Christmas Eve party, and I have to go to that."

"You and Samantha getting pretty close, huh? Well, Junior, I know that you are a gentleman all the time with her, right?"

"Yes, sir. All the time," he said.

"I was seventeen once, and I know what it's like to be in young love. You using rubbers, right? You know I am not ready to be a granddaddy yet, son."

"Ha! Don't worry, I T.C.B, and I wrap it up. Besides she on the pill, so we are covered." He sounded so grown-up and confident stating the facts to me. I was glad that we were able to talk like this about any and everything.

"Well just make sure you treat her right. Never pressure her to do anything and always be gentle. Girls have to be taken care of, and we Sanford men always take care of our women. You got that, son?"

He laughed and went back out of the room.

The news of Donna's new man was a shock, but I was not mad or disappointed. It just made my urge to want to apologize that much stronger. I did not want to have things end like that. I looked at the clock and decided that she was probably at the hospital, so I tried reaching her there. The nurse that answered told me to hold, and she would get her for me.

She came to the phone, and I heard her work voice say, "Hello, this is Donna."

"Hey, Donna. It's me, Kendall. Do not hang up. I wanted to come see you. I need to talk to you in person. What time do you take your lunch today?"

"Kendall, I don't want to see you, and you have nothing to say that I want to hear."

"Donna, please. It has been two months since things went sour. Can I please come see you? I promise I won't bother you again afterward. Please just hear me out."

"I take my lunch at two. Meet me at Old Timers Café on Altamaha."

"Thank you! I will see you at two."

"Alright, see you at two." She hung up the phone without saying goodbye. At least I got her to agree to see me.

I left the office around one o'clock. I told Janie Mae that I was taking a late lunch and probably would not be back in the office until tomorrow. On the drive to Brunswick, I repeatedly rehearsed what I was going to say to her. If she said this, then I would say that in response. I finally got tired of my own thoughts, so I turned up the music and let Lou Rawls speak to me. His words were true. Maybe I should walk in there and tell Donna in song form. She would think I was even crazier than she already did, and I laughed at the thought of it all.

When I arrived at the restaurant, the parking lot was packed with cars. I pulled my pickup truck into a spot that I found around the backside and walked up to the door. Donna must have found a spot up front as someone pulled out because we were walking in at the same time.

"Hey, Donna." I smiled at her, but my warmth was met with a stern look. "I brought these for you," I told her as I handed her two dozen white roses. I wanted to signify that I wanted peace between us.

"Thank you, but you didn't have to get me flowers," she said with a flat tone.

"I know I didn't have to. I wanted to give you flowers." I held the door open for her as we entered the restaurant. The hostess seated us immediately at a booth near the front door. I was surprised that there was even a table available with the number of cars in the parking lot.

We read our menus in silence, and a server appeared at the table almost magically. After placing our orders, Donna looked square at me and asked, "So what did you want to talk with me about, Kendall?"

"Donna, I needed to see you in person so that I could let you know how sorry I am for everything that happened. I would never intentionally do anything to harm you or Kenneth." I started to have that same shameful feeling I had at the hospital when I told my family what had happened.

"Donna, when I woke up in the hospital, I had no idea that you had shot me or why you shot me. They had to tell me what happened. I do remember snorting some blow before I got to your house, but then it all turned into a blur. I was pretty high because my doctor told me that my toxicology report showed levels of cocaine in my system that was enough to kill me."

She sat in silence, staring intently at me, not saying a word. I continued, "Cynthia told me that I had beaten you, but you have to know that I was not myself when I did that. That was the drugs making me act that way. I love you, Donna, and there is no way on this earth that I would ever dream of doing anything to hurt you or my son. Baby, you have to believe me when I say this. I am truly sorry, and that is something that you will never have to deal with from me again. I finished rehabbing, and I am clean from drugs. I know that you will probably never trust me again because what I did was inexcusable, but I hope that you can forgive me."

"Kendall, you are right. I will never trust you again. However, I do want you and Kenneth to get back right. He has been hurting something awful, and for a child to have to witness the man that he holds on a pedestal treating his mother that way… it was not easy for him. These past few months have been no walk in the park for our son. So, what are you going to do to fix this?"

I couldn't come up with a genius answer in such a short amount of time, so I just told the truth. "I don't know how, but I will make it right."

Our food came, and we ate and talked until it was time for her to go back on her shift. She told me about this new boyfriend, and she seemed happy with him. He was the one that answered the phone that day. She asked him to answer because she was waiting on a call from a delivery company that she did not want to miss while she ran next door to get some milk from her neighbor. She wasn't explaining why he answered her phone; it was just a part of our conversation as she told me that she did get the message, but just didn't want to call me back. She agreed that she was going to have Kenneth come out to the house that weekend to stay with us. That would give me time with him to apologize and try to get this behind us.

I could tell we had made some progress with our conversation because she allowed me to hug her good-bye. Even though I was used to kisses, I would settle for whatever she was willing to give me.

Chapter 13

The humidity was fading, and the heat was now tolerable as the sun began to set. Graduation started at eight o'clock, and families began to fill the stadium for the ceremony as soon as the gates opened at six. We had to get in to get a good seat near the stage so I could see my sons walk across the stage. Kendall Jr. and Kenneth would walk across the stage to get their high school diplomas, and all three sides of the family would be there to cheer them on. I was so glad that Donna changed her mind about Kenneth going to school in Darien so that he and Junior could be together. She did not let him live with us, but she was okay with school. The distance to the high school here and the school in Brunswick were the same distance from her house. So, we worked it out where she would drop him off to school in the morning, and I would drop him off at home in the afternoon. When I bought him a car that made life easier for both of us.

At the stadium, all of our families sat in the same section. Cynthia's family sat in front of her and me. My family was behind us, and right behind them were Donna's people. This was normally how we did it for all the boys' sporting events. No matter the relation, they all cheered for both boys no matter what. I credit this to the way that both women took care of the other child, just as if he was their own since they were little boys. They were rarely apart, but that has changed a little now that Junior has a serious girlfriend.

Kenneth is a different story. None of us could keep up with him. Every time we asked, there was a different little girl. I told them both, no babies and to be responsible. I felt that I needed to tell them and kept telling them because no one told me about protection until much later.

I was proud of the boys for making it to this milestone. Kenneth and I had come to terms over the Christmas break. After talking it through, we were back to our normal relationship. I was glad because they were going off to college in the fall, and I needed him to know that his father loved him. I reassured him that I was not the monster that he saw that one night. Since both boys were good at football, they managed to get scholarships to UGA up in Athens. We were all surprised, but I suspect that their uncle might have had something to do with it. He had a great pro career, and was still influential in the world of football. He was a legend in Georgia. He would never admit it, but I always had my suspicions.

***

The air smelled of meat cooking over pecan wood on the grill. Music filled the air from the new boom box that I had gotten from Junior and Samantha for Christmas. They had gotten married soon after graduating from college and were expecting my first grandbaby that summer. Junior joined the family business and was doing a great job in the Savannah office working with my brother, Kevin.

Kenneth seemed to be following the same path as his Uncle David. After his third season playing for the St. Louis Cardinals, he landed himself a spot on the Pro Bowl team. I was so proud of both of my sons and how they turned out.

The cookout was set to start at two o'clock, which meant I needed to get the meat ready, or Cynthia was going to be all over me. She was doing everything else, but I was in charge of the most important part of any cookout - the meat. I had ribs, chicken, burgers, hot dogs, and for those that decided to follow Dick Gregory's meal plan, I grilled some veggie kabobs. Cookouts just seemed to make people happy. Maybe it was the food. Maybe it was the drinks. Heck, I don't know what it was. I just know I was looking forward to having everyone over for a good time. I had the spades table set up and ready to go. The kids even had a slip and slide that they could play on if they wanted to. A good time was ready to be had by all.

Whap! I felt a pop on the back of my neck, and that could only mean one thing. My big brother had made it into town. "Kenny Boy! You don't know what you doing on that grill."

"Man! You wish you had skills on the grill like me." I grabbed David and hugged him. I was always happy to see my partner in crime. I looked over his shoulder and saw who must have been my new sister-in-law. Since they eloped, I had not had the pleasure of meeting her before she became family.

"Excuse him. This joker has no manners. I am Kendall, baby brother to this guy." As I reached to hug her, she stuck out her hand for me to shake it. I took it and realized that she was not from the South.

"Kenny Boy, this is my wife, Patty. Patty, this is Kendall."

"Pleasure to meet you. Whatever you are cooking, sure smells delicious," Patty said.

I pointed at Patty while looking at David. "The lady clearly knows the smell of good barbecue."

We were all acquainted when the other guests began to arrive. The day was going well, and everyone was enjoying themselves. The boys were home, and I had the girls up from Savannah. All was well when my kids were with me. The twins were fourteen and heading to high school the next year. They were growing to be such gorgeous young ladies. They were a little more sheltered than my sons were, but it was about time to start teaching them about these little knuckleheaded boys.

I was always open with Junior and Kenneth, but not with Kimberly and Kenley. Those two were special in my book, and all they needed to know was that they were not allowed to have boyfriends. That may sound delusional, but they were my baby girls, and I wanted to keep them that way for as long as I could.

As the evening began to wind down, and most of our guests left. I was in the house with Cynthia talking in the kitchen when Lester came to get me to come out back and smoke a stogie with the fellas. Cynthia kissed me and pushed me on my way out the door. Kevin, Lester, and David were all out under the shed smoking and sipping cognac. They all looked around at one another, so I knew something was up. It felt like an intervention or an ambush.

"Who is going to tell him?" Lester asked the others.

"Tell me what? Did something happen? Is someone dying?" I asked them as I looked from one to the other.

"Well, it's like this. There is a woman who says you are her kid's father," Kevin blurted out.

"That can't be true because I haven't been with anyone except Cynthia and Ava Lynn," I said with my eyebrows narrowing into each other.

Lester was taking the calm approach. "Kenny Boy, the boy is nine years old. Did you step out with anyone nine or ten years ago that could have possibly gotten pregnant?"

Fuck! That was when Cynthia put me out, and I did sleep with quite a few women during that time. Who could it possibly be?

"Who is the mother, and why didn't she come to me with this instead of putting it out in the streets?"

Lester started telling me the story of how he went up to Stephanie's (his oldest girl) class for career day. As he was talking to the kids, he noticed that one little boy looked familiar. Better yet, he looked exactly like Junior, and when he asked him his name, he told him that his name was Lamont and his mother's name was Kathie Cundiff. He said the last name told him that there was no relation, but he still felt like this resemblance was too strong.

The more he looked at this kid, he knew he had to be kin to us somehow. While he helped Stephanie clean up after the event ended, he did get a chance to meet Kathie. She told Lester that Lamont was his nephew and that I was his father. She said she did not want anything from me, and to Lester, it seemed like she was somewhat ashamed that she was messing with a married man. He wasn't sure if she was telling the truth or not. What he did know was that she knew Lester and I were brothers and that she said that he was my son.

I sat silently as my brother was finishing his story. All the while I was screaming in my head *SHIIIIITTTTTT! Kathie, dammit. You could have told me something.*

***

When everyone left, and Cynthia and I were getting ready for bed that evening, I shared with her what Lester told me about the son that may or may not be mine. She told me that if I had a child in the world that I needed to be the man that she knew I was and take care of my responsibilities. It happened during the time that we were apart, so this news was a little easier for her to swallow. Reaching the age of forty-five certainly calmed me down. At twenty-something, I would have jumped up during the cookout just when I was told the news and run out to find Kathie. I would have made her explain why she had not told me about a child I had fathered. I would have been in full rage, which would have made it a not so good meeting. Instead, I realized it was best to think about everything Lester told me before talking to Kathie.

Almost a month had gone by when I received a return phone call from Kathie. I was starting to think that I was going to have to get a lawyer involved to help sort out the allegations of paternity, but she finally came around.

"Hello, Kendall. This is Kathie. Sorry, it has taken me so long to return your call."

"Hey, Kathie. Thank you so much for calling me back," I told her in my coolest of cool voices.

"I figured that you would be giving me a ring after I talked to your brother up at the school. I really don't know why I decided to tell him that Lamont was his nephew. I hadn't planned to tell anyone, but for some reason when he asked I just-" I interrupted her in mid-sentence.

"Kathie, can I meet you someplace? I think this conversation would be better in person."

"Sure, you can come over any time tomorrow morning."

"Are you still off Altamaha in the house on Glenwood?"

"Yes, still here in the same place as before."

"I will be there at about 9:30 tomorrow morning then, okay?"

We both agreed to the time and hung up the phone. I told Cynt that we had arranged to meet, but I was not crazy enough to tell her that I was going to this woman's house. Cynthia and I both agreed that I needed to ask Kathie for a DNA test since this was during my days of drug use, and I wasn't a hundred percent sure that he was mine.

I am not sure why I was so nervous about asking Kathie for a DNA test for her son. Of all of my children, I never even questioned any of them being mine. I knew when I was with their mothers, how many times and how I was with them if you wanted to be specific. During the time that Kathie would have gotten pregnant was not one of the better times in my life. Rather, it was one of the lowest, and sometimes I wish that I could go back and erase many of the things that I did, especially all of the things that hurt the people who loved me the most. Well, it looked like the DNA test would just be one more thing to add to my list of shit that I have done. Talk about a reminder of your past.

I am just glad that I never got that new AIDS thing that the news was always calling the new American crisis.

When Cynthia found out drug users got AIDS, that was all she needed to hear to make me go get a test done. I was scared shitless waiting for the results, but they came back negative. I was on cocaine, and the doctor said that the people that got it was mostly heroin users back then because they were sharing needles. I went to rehab and kicked that habit before these fools started shooting up crack cocaine. I guess if I had to choose between AIDS or a baby, I would gladly take the kid any day. I think God is funny like that. You are going to live, but BAM! You gotta pay child support for the next 18 years. The only good news was since she did not tell me, I probably would only have nine years left to pay.

When I finally met Lamont, or Monty as we called him, I had no doubts that he was definitely a Sanford. When I met Kathie at her place, we both agreed that it was best that I not meet him until we had the results from the DNA test. She and Monty had their bloodwork done at the Jacksonville Hospital on a Thursday and I went to the same clinic on Friday, so that we did not run into one another. The results took about three weeks to come back, but when they did, it said I was 99.999% the child's father. The doctor said that looking at the results, I had more DNA markers than Kathie, so he was mine without any doubt.

Kathie eased me into Monty's life. We had our first meeting one weekend at her house. Kathie introduced us, and she asked him who he thought I was. He looked up at me with tears in his eyes and asked, "Are you my daddy?" I will never forget that moment as I said a proud "yes." We both just hugged one another, and I apologized for not being there the first few years of his life. I assured him that I was there, and we would spend lots of time getting to know one another.

He was excited by the fact that he had brothers, especially one that was a professional football player, a new niece or nephew on the way this summer, and two sisters that were about to be in high school next year. You could tell that he had been missing a part of himself, and now, thanks to a chance meeting, that was all about to change.

I did ask Kathie why she didn't tell me that I had a child.

"Kendall, I figured like this. You were a man with money, and you and me were just a passing thing. I knew that you never intended to be with me for real. I also knew that you were married. Although I did get involved with you, I felt bad about being with another woman's husband. I just didn't feel right about it. I knew who your people were, but you never really knew much about me, so it was easy for the word not to get out.

"It was not the right thing to do, but you can't change the past, can you? I am just glad that he now has the answer to the question that he has recently been asking so much. He now knows who his daddy is."

I had to ask her, "So if he hadn't been asking about his father, would you still not have said something when Lester asked you?"

"I'm still not sure why I divulged all of my truth to your brother that day. All I can say is that the stars aligned, and my truth was finally told. To be honest, if I hadn't met your brother that day, I probably would still be holding that little secret forever."

"Well I am glad my brother saw the resemblance and was his normal pushy self and started asking questions, or I never would have known about my son," I told her.

We gave a cordial goodbye, and I left with a shared plan with Kathie of how to integrate Monty into the lives of his Sanford family.

Chapter 14

Cynthia was sitting in front of a box fan with only her bra on when I got home. This was a strange sight, as I had never seen her do anything like this. She was normally the person with blankets wrapped around her. She always stayed cold. "Babe, are you running a fever or something? Why are you sitting in front of the fan like that?" I asked her.

She quickly responded, "The change, man. The change."

Oh, I remember when mama went through the change. It was as if she could never get cool, and was always yelling for someone to get her some water. Lawd, I hope this woman wasn't about to try and freeze us to death in this house, too. Mama used to adjust the temperature on her window unit as low as it would go, and she still would not be cool. Daddy wasn't around to see it, but poor Janie Mae had to endure it all alone.

"Do you need for me to get you something? I can go get you some ice cream. That might help cool you off," I said as I stopped putting my stuff down in case I had to go back out.

"YES! That would be good. Butter Pecan, please."

I turned around and headed back for my truck. When I got to the store, I found the ice cream in the freezer. As I was looking through the glass door, I saw one of the old drug dealers from back in the day out of the corner of my eye. He looked so bad that I almost did not recognize him. It looked like he started using what he was dealing, and it had taken a hold of him bad. He spotted me, and so I had to hear his shit.

"Is that you, Kendall? Nigga dat is you! Come here, man! How you been? Let me holla at you real quick," he said through some crusty, cracked lips. They had a crusty white film with hints of red dried up blood deep in the crevices. I knew that I was about to be asked for some cash to help him satisfy his next hit. I had a few rules in my life, and one of those rules was never give money to people to contribute to their misery.

"Hey man, how has everything been going with you? Long time no see," was all I could muster up. I could not call his name to mind, so I just gave a generic greeting.

"Say, man, you got twenty dollars I could hold? I'm about to take this gal out and try and get me a little piece younahwhaimsayin? My money a little funny, though. Can you help ya boy out?"

I assessed the lie but did not respond harshly. I just changed it up on him. "I see. Well, what I can do is get you something to drink and eat. Go grab a drink and something to eat and meet me up at the counter, alright?"

"You alright with me, playboy. I'm coming right now," he said.

Once I paid for all of our items, I fist-bumped him and got in my truck. I looked to the Lord and thanked Him for delivering me from that demon. I had never been the most religious man, but I knew for sure if it had not been for some of God's divine interventions that would have been me in that store begging. I bounced back, and nothing would ever make me go back to do drugs again. I headed home to satisfy my wife's hot flashes, and with any luck, satisfy some of my own desires.

It was a typical steamy summer Thursday morning in Savannah, and I was in town for my weekly meeting. Also, I would get to spend time with Ava Lynn and the girls. At about 9:45, I got a call from Junior telling us that Samantha was in the hospital, and the baby was on the way. I called Cynthia, who was in Darien, to tell her the news that Samantha was in labor. She immediately jumped in her car and headed up to Savannah so she could be one of the first people to meet her new grandbaby. Me? I stayed at work. I was not interested in being at the hospital doing all of that waiting for the baby to come. There was a lot of work to be done since business was booming more than ever, so I finished up for the day before heading over to the hospital.

Kimberly was already at the office with me because she was working as summer help in the Savannah office. When we knocked off for the day, instead of heading straight home, I called Ava Lynn to let her know that Kim-Kim (that's what we called Kimberly) and I would be going to the hospital. I could tell Ava wanted to come to the hospital too, but she knew Cynthia would be there, so she did not push the issue. Cynthia was fine knowing I was with Ava Lynn when I was not home because she understood that I was in love with her. Cynthia also loved the twins dearly. However, she did draw the line at having to be in her presence. The twins were at our house in Darien quite frequently, especially during the summer, and Cynthia was always happy when they came down. One day I asked her why she wasn't friendly towards Ava Lynn in the same manner that she was with Donna. She said that it was a woman thing, and she really could not explain it to me. I could not figure it out, but after that, I never approached that subject again. The way things were was peaceful among us. We just continued to move around in the special way our family did.

When Kim-Kim and I approached Samantha's room, we could hear laughter and squeals of joy coming out of the door. There was a big blue ribbon on the door that read, "It's a boy." Hot damn! Another Sanford man had been born into this world. That made me a little happier. One less thing to worry about. These girls were definitely different than raising these boys, and I sometimes think I just spoiled them too much. Oh well, that is what daddies do with little girls. Well, I know I did it. There he was wrapped up so tight. He reminded me of a football with hair.

"Congratulations, daughter," I said, kissing Samantha on the forehead. Junior was standing with his chest all stuck out like the proud papa. I grabbed him and hugged him very tight.

"Another Sanford man. So, what are you all going to name him?" I asked.

Samantha answered. "We are going to call him Tre."

"That's just his nickname. He is named after some legends. Kendall Sanford the Third," Junior told me.

"Well, the legacy continues. Thank you, son." I patted him on the shoulder. Junior naming the baby Kendall meant a lot more to me than my son could have ever imagined. It truly felt like a part of me would live on. I started to become choked up, but I did not have time to get emotional because I heard a loud thump to my left. I looked down at the floor, and Cynthia had fallen out cold in the middle of the hospital room.

It was as if time stood still. I thought, *As one life enters, one life leaves. I know the Lord would not take my wife while in the hospital meeting our grandbaby. This cannot be happening. Why, why, why, why, why?*

"DAD! Help me get Mama up!" Junior yelling at me snapped me out of the trance.

There were nurses flying in trying to see about Cynthia, and all I could do was be a helpless bystander. I helped Junior load her into the wheelchair that they had brought in, and then got out of the way to let the medical professionals work.

Twenty minutes felt like an eternity. They wheeled Cynthia to the emergency department and did not let us go in with her. My brother-in-law, Theo, was on duty that night. We asked him to go back and see what he could find out for us. Apparently, what was reported back to us was that Cynthia had only blacked out because her blood sugar dropped too low. She was out for about ten minutes before they got her to come back around.

When they finally let me in her room to see her, she was propped up on the bed with an IV coming out of her arm. I smiled at her and said, "Hey, Cynt. You really gave all of us a scare just now. How are you feeling?"

"I'm so sorry to scare you. I do not know what came over me. I remember getting really hot. Then the next thing I knew, it went black."

"Well, I found Theo, and he told us that it looked like it was a drop in your blood sugar." I stopped when I heard the curtains rustle. I turned around and saw a massive man in scrubs enter the area that we were in.

"Hello, I am Dr. Holiday. That was quite an episode that you had back there. I don't know if anyone has ever been so excited about visiting a baby that they passed out on us," he joked. We both chuckled, but it was only to be polite. He kept talking, "Well Mrs. Sanford it looks like we just need to keep you in here on fluids for just a little while. We did a blood draw, and your sugar levels were a little off. Can you tell me if you are a diabetic?"

"No, I have never been told that I was diabetic. I did try this new diet lately. So sometimes I do get a little lightheaded, but I just want to lose a few of these pounds that I picked up recently." Cynthia was using her voice that she only used when she was talking to white people. I laughed at her all the time because she never realized she was doing it.

The doctor continued to quiz her. "When was your last period?"

"Well, I believe I am premenopausal. I have been suffering from hot flashes. Actually, I was just telling my husband that I felt a really strong hot-flash right before fainting."

The doctor had this puzzled look on his face and decided to ask the question differently. "So, would it be safe to say that you haven't had a period in a month or two?"

"The last cycle that I had was around the end of April. So, yes, maybe two months or so ago. My cycles have been irregular for a while. Maybe for the last six months. My gynecologist said that I was in the beginning stages of menopause, and that was to be expected." Cynthia was so matter-of-fact with her statement, but this doctor still had a very weird look on his face.

"Well, Mrs. Sanford, I have some good news and some bad news. The good news is you can stop following that diet. I have deemed it medically unnecessary, and it will bring harm to you if you do not stop. The bad news is you are not going to be successful with your weight loss efforts. Well not for the next six or seven months anyway. Once you deliver this baby that is in your belly, you can go back to battling the bulge." Dr. Holiday just stood there staring at us with our jaws dropped.

"I'm sorry. What do you mean deliver this baby?" Cynthia could hardly finish her sentence. Her face turned the color of that sheet on the bed that she was sitting on.

"Mrs. Sanford, breathe." The machines that she was connected to started chirping and making all sorts of noises. Dr. Holiday called out to her again. "Mrs. Sanford, I need you to breathe slowly." Now he was placing the oxygen mask over her nose. Cynthia mimicked the doctor's breathing pattern and started inhaling the oxygen, which made her chest go up high. Then it lowered as she let that air out. The machines finally calmed down just as Cynthia did.

"You are really making me earn my money today, aren't you? First, you faint from low blood sugar. Now, your blood pressure and heart rate skyrocketed. For both of our sakes, let's get you a Valium," he said.

A nurse came in and gave Cynt the Valium and was told to monitor her closely for fluctuations in her vitals.

Cynthia looked at me with concern in her eyes. "A baby? I thought I was done with that part of my life. We are both forty-five years old, and we have a new grandbaby in this very hospital."

"What is that you're always telling me? God won't put more on you than you can handle? Looks like we just got one more thing to handle," I told my wife as I gave her hand a reassuring squeeze.

She smiled at me, and her face softened. I looked at her and said, "I better go let the kids know that you are alright. Are you okay with me telling them about the pregnancy?"

"Sure. Let someone other than us be shocked for a little while." She laughed it off, and I disappeared behind the curtain to go find the family.

***

"Shut up!" That was Kim-Kim's very loud response to hearing the news that Cynthia was pregnant. At least she had a verbal reaction. Junior just looked plain ol' confused. They were all happy to hear that Cynthia was doing fine, but shocked to learn about why Cynthia fainted.

After delivering the news to the kids, I returned to the ER to sit with Cynthia for a little while longer. Kevin and Lou stopped by the hospital to visit the new parents and their new nephew. Cynthia was not in any shape to drive, so I asked Kevin to take Kim-Kim home, and I drove Cynthia over to Junior's house. She had planned to stay and help the first week that Samantha came home with the baby. Margie, Samantha's mom, would come and stay a few weeks. It seemed a little weird for the husband's mother to be there first, but Margie liked to travel, and she had a trip to Africa planned out and paid for before we even found out the kids were pregnant. So, it just so happened to work out this way.

I had planned to be in Savannah that night, but instead of going over to Ava Lynn's, I stayed with Cynthia to make sure she was fine throughout the night. Ava Lynn understood when I let her know I was not coming over, and she sent Kenley over with dinner for both of us.

Kenley was my shy child. The older she got, the more she came out of her shell. When I answered the door, she gave me our customary daddy-daughter handshake and hug, and then asked, "Is it true I am having a new baby sister or brother?"

"Yes, we just found out earlier that Cynthia is pregnant. Come on in so you can go back and say hello." I closed the door and walked back to the den where Cynthia was lying on the couch.

"Hey, Ma Cynt! How are you feeling?" Kenley asked as she walked over to the couch and sat next to her hip. These two had a special bond, and Cynthia always spoiled her. "When Kim-Kim told me what happened about you fainting and then finding out you were pregnant, that was almost a double heart attack I had."

"Chile, hush your mouth. You sound just like an old woman with that heart attack talk," Cynthia teased her. "Enough about me. You didn't get to meet your new nephew yet. He is such a beautiful baby. I tell you he may be the prettiest baby boy this family has seen yet."

Everyone always said that the Sanford kids all looked the same when they were born. *Big ole yellow babies with perfectly round heads* is usually the description, and it is quite accurate. We will see in a few months with my next baby if it still holds true. I thought that we were done having kids. I had resigned myself to being a grandfather, but now it looks like we will have another one to raise. I would have put my money on Ava Lynn getting pregnant before Cynthia since she was going through the change and all. Humph! The story of my life. Shit never went how I expected, but it always turned out to be okay.

***

119

Time came and went, and before we knew it, we were at home with our new baby girl, Karissa Joy. She gave Cynthia the devil coming into this world. If her birth was any indicator of things to come, Cynthia and I both needed to get ready because we were in for a ride. The last time I had to do any of this baby stuff was 15 years before her with the twins, and Cynt had been out of practice much longer since our son together was a grown man with a baby of his own.

We eased our way back into things. My mother-in-law came by every day to help with the baby while I was at work, and once I got home, she would have dinner cooked and head back to her house. She was a beautiful baby, but my genes did not take hold to this baby like the others. Even Lamont looks just like a Sanford, and he did not even carry our last name. There is a first time for everything, and I guess Cynthia had to win at something.

Chapter 15

Karissa Joy grew up so fast. Seems like we blinked and she was a teenager in high school. Cynthia came into the den where I had fallen asleep on the couch. I felt her shaking my arm to get me to wake up. "Kendall, have you heard from Karissa?" Cynthia asked, sounding worried.

"Nah, babe, what time is it?" I woke up a little more and looked at the clock to see that it was 1:30 in the morning. This was strange that she was not home because she had never missed curfew. A few hours earlier, we were at the football game to watch her cheer, and afterward, we let her go get pizza with her friends. She knew she had to be in the house on time, no exceptions. I figured she was out with that boy, Tajai. And what the hell kind of name is Tajai anyway? She had always been responsible, but I guess she was at that age where she felt the need to test her limits. Cynthia was pacing so fast I could not tell if she was worried or mad.

"Cynthia, did you try her cellphone?"

"Yes, but it just rings and rings with no answer."

Then the phone rang. We knew it was her. Cynthia answered the phone, "Karissa, where are you, young lady?"

Whoever was on the other end could not have been Karissa because there was no yelling or chastising. When she put the phone on the cradle, she started to tear up.

"Cynthia! Who was it? Who was on the phone?"

"That was the hospital. Karissa was in a car accident. They said they were doing what they could, but they have to transport her to the trauma unit in Savannah at Memorial," Cynthia sobbed. "Kendall, the other kids that were in the car with her didn't make it. They are dead." That was when she became undone. She was full-blown hysterical, and I was not really in a state of mind to calm her down. I just wanted to get to my daughter, but Savannah was an hour drive away. I got on the phone and called Junior. He jumped right into action. He told me that he would head straight to the hospital.

We dressed and hurried as much as possible to get on the road. Junior called us about fifteen minutes after we had hung up from him the first time saying that he had arrived at the hospital and the helicopter had not landed yet. Cynthia and I started the trek up I-95. She cried and prayed the entire way. I was glad that I had stopped to fill up before the football game because I think Cynthia would have tried to make me drive on fumes rather than waste time getting to our baby. We got about fifteen minutes up the road when Junior called my cellphone and said that he heard the helicopter land. The nurses told him that they would take her straight to trauma and that he would need to wait in the waiting area. Someone would come out to give an update on her progress as soon as she was stable.

"Junior, we are almost there. Thank you, son, for keeping your mama and me posted. See you in a few minutes." I hung up the phone and kept my eyes trained on the road in front of me. I do this drive all the time, but tonight seemed as if this was the longest road trip I had taken in my life.

Exactly one hour after leaving our driveway, I was pulling into the parking lot of Savannah Memorial Hospital. No one was stationed at the information desk at the entrance, so we had to follow the signs until we found the trauma unit. Whenever someone is shot, they always show the sign that reads "trauma unit" on the news. I never expected to be here to see the sign in real life, but here I am waiting to hear the fate of my little girl. I guess we could be considered lucky because the other parents' phone calls went a little different from ours.

There were four kids in the car, and Karissa was the only one who survived. We knew that she was alive, but we didn't know was how close she was to death. All that we had been told so far was that she was fighting for her life. We waited for two hours before someone came out to talk to us.

A white boy in blue scrubs came into the waiting area. He looked straight at us because we were the only people in the room. He waited before coming over. Then about three seconds later an older white man entered the room, and they both walked over to us with stoic looks plastered across their faces.

"Hello, I know that you all have been out here a while waiting to hear what is going on with your daughter. She is stable right now, but she is in an induced coma due to the injuries that she incurred. Karissa suffered two broken legs, a broken arm, and a collapsed lung. Oh, she is a fighter that one." He let a smile cross his lips. "She was able to tell the flight nurse her name, and she was very matter-of-fact in saying, 'When they get to the hospital, let my Mama and Daddy know I am doing alright.'"

Cynthia was always brimming with questions, so this exchange did not call for her to change up her normal MO. "Thank you, doctor, but what exactly does an induced coma do to help our daughter?" She was using her code-switching voice for this one.

"Well ma'am, it allows for her to rest and not feel the pain. The main reason is to reduce the risk of brain damage. We utilize this method quite frequently, and it is safe if that is what you are worried about," he responded calmly.

"How long will she have to be in this coma?"

"She will be monitored, and when the risks are diminished, we will stop the utilization of the drug that is making her sleep, and she will come out of it. Have you ever had a surgery where they put you under? Think of it that way. Just like when you woke up, she will wake up by the same mechanism." His examples were actually making sense to me.

I assume that this made sense to Cynthia as well because her next question was simply, "Doc, when can I see my baby?"

"We are getting her settled into ICU. A nurse will come let you know when you can go back." He smiled at us in the way doctors do to try to reassure you.

The three of us stood in the center of the room and hugged each other. Cynthia was still crying, and we just held on to her to comfort her as best we knew how.

Later that morning, we were able to go in one at a time to sit with Karissa. Most of the family, along with Karissa's friends, filled the ICU waiting room. We limited who all we would let back to immediate family and her best friend, Monique. The entire day was filled with folks stopping in to visit. When the hospital visiting hours ended, everyone bid us farewell and left for the evening.

I left and went to take a shower and change clothes over at Ava Lynn's house. I had a full closet of clothes there. It was my second home. I stayed there for almost an hour before heading back to the hospital to relieve Cynthia so that she could shower. As we were sitting in the waiting room, we got a visit from another doctor to tell us that her blood count was slowly dropping and Karissa needed a blood transfusion. They said that blood supplies were low at their blood bank and asked if we minded donating blood. We both went to let them draw bags of our blood to help save our daughter.

Cynthia was deep in prayer when the doctor came back to ask us some questions. The first thing that came to my mind when he came in with that look on his face was *Lord, not my baby girl.*

"Mr. and Mrs. Sanford, I want to apologize for not asking more questions before the blood draw. I needed her birth parents to donate blood so that we could have a match. I did not express that before, and I had you give blood that we cannot use. Do you know who her birth parents are? Maybe they can come down and donate," the doctor told us with a very serious demeanor.

"What are you talking about? We are her birth parents. I know that we are older, but we had her late," I told her.

"Oh, I see. My apologies. Do you know of anyone in the family who we can test to see if they are a match to donate blood to Karissa?" he asked. "Her numbers are falling fast, and our blood bank supplies are depleted. We need to try and get her blood as quickly as possible."

"I will call her siblings to see if I can get them to come down here to see if they are matches," I told the doctor. She walked away with a look of remorse on her face.

I looked Cynthia dead in the eye and asked, "Who was it, Cynthia?"

Cynthia did not answer. She just stared at me with the rims of her eyes rapidly filling with water. I repeated my question, angrier this time. "Who the fuck was it, Cynt!"

"It was a long time ago. It was a mistake. She is OUR daughter, and right now, I am not up to dealing with this scenario. We are both too old, and I, for one, am not in the frame of mind to hash this out with you in the hospital waiting room!" Cynthia stated. Her eyes looked full of emotion, but her voice was steady and matter of fact. She was more worried about how Karissa was doing than she was about me being angry. Now, I guess I could understand why she felt that way, but I certainly felt like I was hit by a ton of bricks then.

"Let me go call the kids and see who might be able to come down and donate. I'll be outside if you need me."

So many thoughts raced through my mind all at once. How could I be so blind not to know that she was not my biological child? In all of my years being married to Cynthia, I had never wanted to hurt her or bring harm to her. Oh, but then, I wished that I could beat her ass for lying to me all these years. I do not know who I am madder at. Cynthia for cheating on me, or myself for trusting her so much. Thing is, it had crossed my mind once or twice that she may have stepped out on me, but I would always chalk that up to my mind playing tricks on me. Fuck! How could she? I raised and loved Karissa. She was my baby girl, and I loved her to the moon and back. There was nothing anyone could say or do to change that fact. What the fuck was I supposed to do with that information?

"Are you alright, sir?" a little nurse asked me. I was pacing in front of the door mumbling to myself.

"What? Oh, yeah, yeah. I'm fine. Just a little shaken up, that's all." She accepted that answer and moved on her way.

I walked to the parking garage and sat in the car so that I could gather my thoughts before calling all the kids. The ones who lived in town were there within an hour. Junior came and brought Tre' along with him to see if he could be a possible donor. Kim-Kim and Kenley both showed up together with their big brother. Kenneth had caught the first flight out that he could get once he heard the news.

When I saw all those faces, I knew that Cynthia and I had to put on a strong front and could not give any hints that we were not on the best of terms right now. Cynthia came up with some excuse to tell the kids about my medication making me ineligible and her not being a match to donate. Of all the kids that got their blood tested, the twins and Lamont were able to donate to their little sister. Good thing that all three were able to donate because the way the doctor made it sound, she was fading away fast. We remained prayerful that she would pull through and get back to living her teenage life.

That night in the waiting room after the kids donated, we sent everyone home so that they could get some rest and promised that we would let them all know of any changes. We joked that if she sneezed too hard, we would call them.

I leaned over to Cynthia and whispered, "No one needs to know except us. I don't even want to know who you was fucking around with. Just tell me one thing. Is it done?"

She nodded her head to signify to me that it was done. I vowed that I would put it out of my mind that night and never let the fact that she was with another man bother me.

***

Karissa Joy. Her name expressed exactly how we felt when she came into this world by accident (literally). She gave us a scare with that car accident, but she pulled through that like a champ. The doctors where very surprised at how quickly she recovered. My high school graduate was heading off to college. I was against her going so far away from her family. However, I was outvoted as usual. We drove her up to Virginia to drop her off at Hampton University. I had done this plenty of times before, but this time it seemed to sting a lot more.

While we were there, we went to one of Kenneth's pre-season games. His team was playing against the Redskins in the final game before the start of the regular season. He played for a long career, longer than most guys did. When he finally retired from being a player, he moved over into coaching the very next season. He told us that during his last year, he was coaching the younger cats on the team, and they seemed to listen to him pretty good. It was just a no brainer. He had the respect of the coaches already, and it just so happened a position opened up at that exact time. Most guys have to coach high school and college to build their coaching resume, but this just happened for him.

I think the other reason that Karissa knew she could go all the way to Virginia was that she had a big brother there if she needed him. Also, Tre', her nephew, who was more like a brother, would be a sophomore there this year. When she spent homecoming weekend with him last fall is when I think she was completely sold that this was the school for her. We are all glad that we had family in place just in case there is an emergency. Kenneth served as a father away from home for Tre', and now we can add Karissa Joy to his duties.

Chapter 16

September rolled around, and our house had been so quiet that we did not know what to do with ourselves. I had semi-retired from the company, and Junior was running the majority of our operations. My brothers and I remained on the board, but when it came to the day-to-day operations, we were no longer involved too much. The company provided so much for our family over the years. We were all proud of what we built. Pops kicked it off, my brothers and I made the dream a reality, and our children were now taking us into the new millennium. However, I was getting bored sitting here looking at Cynthia day in and day out. I guess Cynthia was feeling the same way about me.

"Kendall, what do you think about taking a trip to Europe? Inez has a group going, and I think it would be fun for us to get out and see some of this world before we get too old," Cynthia said shoving a brochure in my face for a couples getaway. You fly into a city, then get on a boat for a cruise, then fly back to the states. I figure a cruise out of Jacksonville or one of the ports in Florida would be much cheaper, but I was willing to entertain this notion of traveling if only to keep the peace because she would never let me hear the end of it if I didn't at least listen.

"Okay, what's this all about? I hope this ain't one of your church trips that's gonna try to make me some super Christian. You know I can't deal with all that mess," I told her.

From when we first got married, she was a member of her father's church. I would go when it was a necessary family event, but I never joined. I am a believer, but that holier than thou shit is for the birds, and at that church, they were full of sanctimonious folks. I preferred the smaller church that my family went to for years. That's were my membership lived since I was a little boy when Mama took us to church with her every Sunday. There have been quite a few pastor changes since that time, but my name never came off the rosters. I kept it that way by sending my tithe and offerings. That kept me in good standings, I guess. I may not go often, but I do know the Lord. However, I did not want to spend a vacation with a bunch of church hypocrites. If I am spending money, I need to be able to enjoy myself without being watched by judgmental eyes.

Cynthia went on to tell me that it was for couples that were over the age of fifty, and they would have workshops about marriage and different things that are going on in this season of our lives. There would only be one session per day, and she wanted to go more for the experience. Cynthia said that once we were on the ship, we wouldn't have to go to any sessions if I didn't want to. I knew that was a lie from the moment it crossed her lips. She went on and on until I finally asked about the cost. The price wasn't bad, so I told her we could go.

It seemed like the time flew by because we were walking up the gangway before I could blink an eye. Cynthia had been shopping and packing for the past few months. She had not been this excited about anything in a long time. She researched every aspect of this trip. She was prepared enough for the both of us. All I did was show up. I did not have the energy or the desire to be bothered. That is what I had a wife for, right? She paid attention to all those small details so that I didn't have to. We had been married for over forty years, and I did not plan to change anything at this point in my life, especially when it was working. So, she got us all set to go.

I can admit that everything was first class, and I enjoyed myself. Some of our friends joined in, and I knew a few of the fellas that we were traveling with, so that made those group dinners fun. Then I had some guys to smoke cigars and shoot the shit with while the women were in the spa. Even the marriage sessions were decent, and I felt like I learned a great deal about myself.

On our last full day on the boat, after leaving lunch, I whispered to Cynthia, "Thank you for getting everything together for us to come on this trip. This has been such a good time."

The biggest smile came across her lips, and I could see that she was happy because I enjoyed myself. She leaned in and whispered back, "Thank you for being such a good sport and agreeing to come. I love you, Kendall."

That last night was a big last hurrah for our group. They had all you can drink beverages in a private dining room just for the couples in attendance. Between the wine and liquor, I think most of us forgot that we were the "over 50" crew. There was so much laughter and shit-talking you would have thought we were all back in our twenties. Then we started trying to have a meaningful conversation, which was even more interesting because everyone had been drinking.

"Say, Kendall. I feel like over the past week we have gotten close enough that I can ask you something that I have wanted to ask you for a real long time," Wilton said a little louder than he knew that he was.

"Okay, what's that, Wilt?" I figured it could not be too serious since we have known each other for so many years. Our wives were best friends, so we were forced together due to their relationship.

"Kendall, how in the world did you manage to keep up the marriage with Cynthia here for so long. I just knew y'all wouldn't make it this long. If I had kept other women the way that you do, shiiddd. Deloris would have shot me. I would be sitting here dead." The whole table burst out into laughter. It was apparent from the response that everyone had discussed this in some form or other over the years.

"I can admit that to the unknowing eye, our marriage was not traditional in a few ways." I stopped and looked at Cynthia to see if I could gauge how she felt about this conversation so that I could steer it in the right direction. I could tell that she was a little embarrassed. I tried to reign it back in. "Cynthia and I love each other, and that is how we managed to make it last this long. She understands me, and that is all that matters. What we got don't need to make sense to nobody except us."

Deloris chimed in and said, "That's right, Kendall. Cynthia has been my best friend for as long as I can remember, and she is a happy woman because of you." She smiled very hard at me, and as I was turning away from her, I caught the death glare that she shot at her husband. I wondered what the hell kind of pillow talk those two had been having about us. I figured Wilt would have thought it best to shut up about it. Then again, I thought wrong because he decided to keep it going. He was always that type to say just a little too much when he had a few drinks, so this did not surprise me.

Wilton turned his attention to another couple. "Chuck, what do you think about this? Do you think that Jackie would allow you to have another woman that you have a whole other family with, then come home to her house and lay up with her?"

Chuck moved to Darien after he was appointed the new police chief back in 1984. I guess he was a real-life Virgil Tibbs. He was dating Jackie, but she was still living in her hometown. They dated long distance for a few years, and once they finally got married, she moved to town. Our wives started hanging out together when she moved to town and were in the same circles.

Chuck just looked at Wilton and replied, "That is that man's business. I don't think one way or the other about it."

Jackie grabbed his arm a little tighter. It was obvious that she was oblivious to this entire conversation. You could tell by the way she was pawing at him that Chuck was due for a great last night onboard.

"Well, I know I couldn't get away with it. That's all I'm saying," Wilton finished and returned to drinking his drink.

I leaned over to Cynthia and whispered, "Do you want to call it a night and go on up to the room? Wilt has reached his limit, and I can't promise my composure if he keeps this shit up."

She said, "You know how he is. He'll be apologetic in the morning for all of this. We were having such a good time. We are not going to let him ruin our last night on board."

I followed Cynthia's lead, and she was right. He eased up, and we had an enjoyable finish to dinner. We all were still feeling like we wanted to keep the fun going, so we went to a 70s music dance party. The DJ was playing all of the old hits that we used to enjoy. When *Brick House* came on, I just knew Deloris was going to dislocate a hip. Cynthia went to the restroom, and I stayed at the table with the drinks. I watched everyone twirl around the floor and thought to myself, *I hope they packed some Bengay because every joint they have will be aching tomorrow morning when it is time to get off the ship.*

My bladder started to get full (alcohol did that to me), so I told one of the other guys that was from our group to watch our drinks and make sure no one took our seats. As I entered the gallery where the bathrooms were, I heard some arguing coming from one of the closed-off rooms. I recognized Cynthia's voice and listened closer to see what was going on.

I overheard a male voice say, "I cannot believe that I have to sit here and listen to this farce of a man talk about how good he has been to you." He continued on, "I would have never agreed to be on the same ship with you and him because this has been pure torture. That is my fault, though, for not asking who was going to be attending. Cynthia, we haven't been together in so long, but I just cannot think about how much I miss you. You know I love you, and the only reason I married her is because I couldn't have you. Tell me you do not miss me. That you don't ever think about us, and what could have been. Tell me, and I will leave this alone and never mention it again."

I could not stand to listen anymore. I walked back to the room and laid down on the bed. I was so angry with so many thoughts running through my mind. He said they had not been together in a "long time." I needed to know when the last time was. Was this who had gotten my wife pregnant? How could I not have known? It was times like those that I want to forget about staying clean and get high. There was no reason why anyone should have to deal with that shit. I had been a good husband. No, I had been a fucking great husband to her. With the exception of that lapse in judgment when she ended up kicking me out, I always took care of home. I was honest, even when I did not want to be, about everything. I did not fuck around on her. She knew it all. This feels as raw as the first time that the doctor said it was not possible for me to be Karissa's father. I said I would not ever bring it up again because she promised that the affair was over, but I heard another man tell my motherfucking wife that he loved her. ARGH! That right there still gets people killed. I knew she had fucked someone else, but damn. I would have never guessed that the self-righteous son of a bitch was someone I actually knew.

I do not know how long I was in the cabin before I heard Cynthia opening the door. I just know that it was not long enough because I was still pissed. Then that voice became clear to me all of a sudden.

"Chuck?" I blurted out. "The motherfucking officer of the peace? That piece of shit?"

Cynthia was caught off guard and just stared at me.

I started shouting. "Answer me, dammit! So, Chuck is the one that you were fucking and got pregnant for?"

Cynthia's eyebrows narrowed, and she whispered, "Keep your voice down. These cabin walls are paper-thin, and you know people are asleep."

I was more hurt because she was worried about the people who were asleep and did not deny what I just accused her of doing.

She was right. It was late, but I wanted us to talk about this. I took a deep breath and started talking very slow and low. I asked her again, choosing my words very carefully. "Cynthia, I just heard you arguing with someone. Was that Chuck that you were arguing with when you left to go the bathroom?"

"Yes, that was Chuck that I was talking to."

"Is he who got you pregnant with Karissa?"

She looked me dead in the eye. "Yes."

I was not real sure what else I wanted to know. Then the question just flew out. "Does Chuck know?"

Still calm, she stated, "No, he does not."

We sat and looked at each other for a while, and then she moved into wife mode and got our small bag ready for departure. She made sure the big bags were packed, tagged, and placed outside the cabin door for pickup. Then she got herself ready and went to bed.

I was still mad, but what was there to do? I was a million miles away from home, and I could not react in the way I wanted to. I was in disbelief that this had blown up in my face, and she was sleeping like nothing happened.

I shook her shoulder because I wanted to talk some more. She sat up and obliged me.

"Cynthia, I know that I said I didn't want to know who it was and promised not to talk about it again after we left the hospital when I found out. You have to understand that I have some questions about this whole thing."

She sat up and told me the entire story from beginning to end. She told me that they met in town one day, and they were talking and just hit it off. She invited him to come to church and worship. They started as casual friends, and she tried to be helpful in getting him settled in the community. Then one week she invited him out to the house to have dinner with us, and I did not come home. I stayed on in Savannah with Ava for a few days. She confided in him about our relationship, and shared how lonely she was with me away. He was lonely too because the girl that he was dating he had left behind.

Their friendship went from friends to lovers over the course of a few months. It was no big deal because he only came around when I was out of town on my weekly visits to Savannah. She took care of his needs, and he took care of hers. She told me that she knew that there was a chance that he had gotten her pregnant, but it was not until the day that we were in the hospital that her notion had been confirmed. After that, I think it brought back the same wave of anger when I first asked her about it at the hospital, so everything else she said sounded like that teacher on Charlie Brown. Wha-wha-wha-wha. I never did fall asleep. I just stared up at the ceiling of our cabin until it was time to get off the ship.

***

We lied our heads off. When my sister-in-law picked us up from the airport in Jacksonville, Cynthia told her about all the wonderful things that we saw while we were in Europe, and about how great the trip and the sessions were. You would never know that we had not spoken a full sentence to each other since we got off the ship. We just went through the motions, and I guess no one noticed because everyone was too tired or too hungover to care.

There were a few things that I was grateful for on our way traveling back. The first being the new earphones that I had gotten for my birthday gift from Kim-Kim. The second thing was that Chuck and Jackie were not on the same flight home with us. They were set to stay a few more days and tour a few more countries before heading back to the states. I swear I am not so sure about what I would have done. I wasn't ready to face that bastard yet. I liked my freedom, and I cannot promise that I wouldn't have been sent to prison for homicide. He and I never really got along. We just tolerated each other because our wives ran in the same circles. I originally thought we just did not have anything in common, which is why we didn't care for one another. I couldn't have been more wrong in that aspect since we had the one thing in common that should have been off-limits to every man under the sun except me - sleeping with my wife.

When we got home, I unpacked showered and went straight to bed. I wanted to get my body adjusted to the time change as quickly as possible, and my mind said that sleep was the only way to solve that problem. When I woke up the next day, I was surprised at how long I had slept. When I looked at the clock, it was 12:47 in the afternoon. I had slept for over twelve hours. I looked around the room, but Cynthia was not there. The bedroom curtains were drawn, so the room was dark thanks to the new blackout shades Cynt installed. The scent of that cherry blossom body lotion that she used still lingered in the air so she must not have been gone for too long.

I left the bedroom to find that I was alone in the house, which was fine with me because every time I looked at Cynthia, I got mad all over again as if I just heard the news for the first time. We had been gone on vacation, so there was barely any food in the house because Cynthia did not grocery shop. She said it would all spoil by the time we returned. I dug around in the freezer and found a package of sausage. I fired up my cast iron skillet and fried a couple of links of my favorite Roger Wood sausages. The bread that was in the breadbox didn't have nothing growing on it, so I got two slices and made my sausage sandwich. I topped that bad boy off with some mustard, and I had myself a meal.

Just when I was getting ready to go back upstairs, I heard the garage door going up, which was my signal that Cynthia was back home. She walked into the house, all smiles. I couldn't help but get jealous. I guess I wanted to know what was making her smile so big. Was it Chuck? Did he put that smile on her face, or was it some other dude who I had not found out about yet? I just looked at her, shook my head, and started walking out of the room.

"What is it, Kendall?!" Her sharp questioning caught me off guard.

"I just was wondering what has got you smiling so much this morning? Better yet, *who* has got you smiling like that?" There was a little bit of anger in my tone, but I really didn't care at this point.

"Excuse me! I know that you, Kendall Sanford, do not have the audacity to stand here and question me about being with someone else. I am the wife, who has spent an entire marriage never having you entirely to myself," she said with venom in her voice after every word.

"Cynthia, what are you talking about? I have been your husband. I have been open with you about everything that I have done. When have I ever not taken care of this house, the kids, or you? Don't give me this bullshit about what I do. I have always been open and never ran around on you. You know exactly where I am, and this is what we have been doing. You decided to step outside of our lifestyle and sleep with someone else. Then the cherry on top is that my baby girl is not MINE! Then you want to criticize me for things that we both agreed on. Come on, Cynthia. You fucked up." I could not even look at her from this point. I was not even sure that I could say more without growing angrier.

She started speaking in that slow, steady tone that she uses when she is trying to control her temper. "Do you really think that I liked you going off with Donna when we were first married, or with your Ava Lynn once you reunited? I hate every minute that my husband is away with another woman. Did I accept it? Yes, I did. Because you are my husband. Having you in whatever manner meant more to me than walking away and having no you at all. I love you, Kendall, but let's face it. You have treated me with so much disrespect during the course of our marriage. People always ask me why I put up with you and these other women. Do you realize how embarrassing that is to have everyone know that my man has a whole other household that he is taking care of? I think the only thing good to come out of it all was the children. Those were all my blessings because they are an extension of you. Other women I know would not allow children born outside of a marriage into their house. The way I see it, those children did not have anything to do with your sinful fornicating."

I cut her off right there, "Seriously?!"

"Yes, seriously. You were sleeping with other women for years. Since the very beginning of our relationship. I am just calling it what it is."

"So, you do realize that you too are a sinful fornicating heathen according to what you just called me since you know you had a baby by someone else and let me raise her as my own for sixteen years without me knowing it. Wait, so that makes you a fornicator and a liar."

"Well, then we are just a pair of fornicating liars. When you ran into Ava Lynn again, would you have told me about her if we hadn't ended up at the same place together? Don't forget that you snuck around for months before I found out. Being faithful to your wife was not even an option for you, was it? It wasn't enough that you had Donna and me. You had to add another woman to your roster." The moment she said that last statement I knew that this conversation had come up with some of her girlfriends. Having a "roster" is not something that Cynthia would say. One of her friends must have used that when they were talking about me.

"Cynthia, it is obvious that we are both angry, and we are apparently both feeling some pain over both of our actions in our relationship over the years. I am man enough to admit that I thought I could push my feelings aside and move forward like I didn't know. When we left the hospital, I said that I would not let this thing come up again. Then when I found out that you had been with Chuck, and he was the motherfucker who got you pregnant, I just couldn't let it go. I'm sorry. This has cut me deeper than you can know."

She softened her tone. "Kendall, trust me. I know that pain all too well. You have four kids that I did not birth. I didn't tell you that I had been with Chuck because I did not want you to experience what I had felt over the years. The reason I was with him at all was because I was lonely. Our marriage is a hot mess and way too embarrassing to ever talk about outside of the two of us. Kendall, what are we doing? We are in our sixties now. When will I ever be enough for you? No Ava, no Donna, nobody except you and me? Is it possible for us to ever get to that? Being a happy monogamous couple that loves each other unconditionally no matter what?" She was staring at me, and I felt like the pressure was on me.

"Cynthia, I love you. Always have and always will. If you are asking me what I think you are asking me then-"

She cut me off saying, "Kendall, I am asking you to stop seeing Ava Lynn. I do not want to spend the rest of my life sharing my husband with another woman. So, no need to guess about what I am asking. I am making it plain and clear. STOP. BEING. WITH. AVA LYNN. Be MY husband." The rims of her eyes filled with water. I pulled her in close to me, and I held her tightly in my arms. She wept in my arms for what seemed like forever. Then our healing process began by consummating a new beginning in our marriage.

Chapter 17

It had been over a month, and I had not physically seen Ava. I wanted to honor Cynthia's wishes and try to be the husband that she so desperately needed. However, I could not bring myself to tell Ava about this new development in our relationship. For over thirty years, we had lived and loved with this arrangement, and to spring this on her now just did not seem like the right time. It was not what I wanted, and I am sure that she didn't want it either. Staying away from her had been easy since Ava was in Augusta seeing about her father, who had become very sick.

Dr. Jefferson had grown older and had fallen victim to the same disease that claimed the lives of so many black men - prostate cancer. Ava Lynn was his primary caregiver. She relocated up to Augusta to make sure that everything was okay with her father. She made sure he went to the doctor appointments, took his medicine on time, and put all of his affairs in order. After all, this was her daddy. She always was and would always be a Daddy's Girl, and not a soul would try to dispute that fact.

The twins would stop by Ava's house in Savannah while she was seeing about their grandfather. All three of them were some independent women who definitely knew how to take care of business. Ava Lynn and I raised some great girls, and they took after her so much. Ava Lynn's smarts and business savvy were the things that attracted me to her when we reconnected all those years ago.

When she first left my life, I was not sure how I was going to go on without her. But when she showed up out of the blue one day, I vowed never to let her go again. So just how was I supposed to not have her in my life at all and make Cynthia happy? This was the challenge I faced. When would actually be a good time to tell Ava that my wife said I could no longer see her? I loved Cynthia because she had been my wife and by my side all these years. However, I knew I hadn't gotten past the fact that Karissa wasn't my biological daughter, and she had lied to me for so long.

My oldest brother once asked me, "Kenny Boy, how can you sit here and say you truly love all these women you with?" I know it seems odd, but this was my reality. I loved each of them for their different roles in my life. Things like this were never easy to explain or even understand, but it was my truth. I loved both Cynthia and Ava Lynn, just in different ways.

As I sat in total concentration, I was gearing up to call Ava for our daily check-ins. I was contemplating telling her about Cynthia's new demands that she shared with me. I did not agree with them, so I was not totally sold on it yet, which is why I hadn't said anything.

"Hi, Kendall!" Her voice was a little more chipper today.

"Hey, Ava. How are you today, sweetie? You sound really happy," I told her.

"Well, I have some good news to share. My daddy had a great doctors visit, and he was able to get up and run errands with me this morning," she said almost squealing.

"That is wonderful news. I am glad that Dr. Jefferson is on the upswing."

"We are not out of the woods yet, but his PSA levels and all of his other readings came back in a good range. No signs of metastasis and the doctor feels like the surgery may have gotten it all." She continued telling me about the next phases of treatment and what all had to be done next to get him back to a normal state of health.

"Ava, all of this is such good news. I am so happy to hear this. Now how have you been? Taking care of others can be hard on you. How have you been holding up?" I asked her.

"Well, dealing with Daddy has been hard, but I will tell you that I am happy to be able to do it. I am blessed enough to have a support system in the girls and you to get me through this rough patch."

"We do have some amazing girls, don't we?" You could hear the pride in my voice.

"Yes, we sure do. Kendall, the only thing that is off in my life right now is that I need my man. I need to see you. I know that you never really cared for my parents because of how things went when we were in high school. Do you think you could bring yourself to come up to Augusta and visit me?"

"I don't think I can get away from here. When are you coming back home? I can come to Savannah to see you." *So much for what Cynthia wants,* I thought to myself. The moment she said she missed me that entire notion went out of the window.

"My aunt said she could stay over whenever I needed to run back home for something. I may just have to take her up on that offer," Ava said.

"Alright, then. Let me know when you get it all worked out, and I will be there," I told the love of my life.

"I will let you know what plans I arrange so we can coordinate. Kendall, I can't wait to see you. I love you so much," she told me with honey dripping from her words.

"I love you, too, Ava Baby."

Now what was I going to do? At that instant, my stomach growled, confirming just how hungry I really was. I would have to figure it out once I ate dinner. I hoped Cynthia cooked something good that night so that I could think.

I could not bring myself to end things with Ava Lynn. I did not say anything to Cynthia about my decision one way or the other. Once Ava Lynn nursed her father back to health, she was home on a more consistent basis. She never even knew about Cynthia's request. I just picked up and fell back into my old routine of the days where I would see Ava Lynn in Savannah. Truthfully, we all fell back into our old routines. Cynthia never brought it up so, I just kept on moving about life and doing what made me happy - seeing my Ava Lynn. Deep down, I knew the subject would be sure to rear its ugly head again somehow.

The seasons faded into one another, and my routine had fallen back into a comfortable rhythm. Everyone was happy, or at least content, with the lifestyle that we were living in. It was a warm Sunday afternoon, and Cynthia and I were sitting out on the front porch chewing on some sugarcane when I heard my phone begin to ring. Chewing cane was one of my all-time favorite past times, so whoever it was had better call the house phone or call me back.

I heard the bells chime that Karissa put on there to let me know there was a voice message for me to check. When I finished eating my cane, I went inside and got my phone to check it. There was a number showing up that I didn't have saved. When I called the voicemail, there was a message from a telemarketer saying that I was eligible for an all-expense-paid trip to Sin City, Las Vegas. These telemarketers finally tapped into the cellphone numbers, but I loved to play crazy with them when I did answer.

One time this young girl called me, and I started speaking that real thick Geechee on her. She finally said, "Sir, I don't know what language that is you are speaking, but you have a nice day." Cynthia and I laughed so hard that day. We tried to make a game out of it whenever they called. We competed to see who got the best reaction out of them. Bonus points were given if we could make them curse. I think we got sillier in our old age. The phone rang again with the caller ID showing another number that was not familiar to me.

"HaYellow," I answered with some extra chirp in my greeting.

"Mr. Sanford?" the voice on the other end quizzed.

"Depends, who's asking," I replied.

"Mr. Sanford this is Celeste Hopkins at Memorial Hospital in Savannah. I have you listed as an emergency contact for Ms. Ava Lynn Jefferson. She came in for her annual colonoscopy, but there were some complications during the procedure. We need to have someone who is capable of making medical decisions on behalf of Ms. Jefferson to come to the hospital as soon as possible."

"I will be right there." A wave of red with vivid images of Ava flashed in my mind, and I started running on autopilot again. No matter how many times you get unexpected calls that feeling of numbness still shows up and takes over you completely. I felt this same paralyzing numbness when we got the call about Karissa's accident. It was as if your body knew that it had to move, but your mind could not keep up with what was going on. I often thought people were looney tunes when they would say things like, "It was like I was outside of myself just watching what was happening around me." Well, that was exactly how I felt.

I got to Savannah somehow. I could not even begin to tell you what happened between that phone call and me finding the doctors in the hospital. I must have called the girls to tell them about their mother because when I arrived, they were both already at the hospital. As I walked up, I could see shades of pink in the parts of their eyes that were supposed to be white. I did not want to jump to conclusions, but with this scene, I wanted to brace myself for the worst.

Kim-Kim came over and hugged me very tightly. "Daddy, they said she is in a coma, and they are not sure what caused it."

A tall thin white man who looked only old enough to be barely out of high school came over to us. "Are you Mr. Sanford?" I responded in the affirmative. "Mr. Sanford, I'm one of the doctors here who has been seeing about Ms. Jefferson. She was at her doctor's office for a routine procedure, and her vitals began to fluctuate. They called for an ambulance to have her transported to the emergency room. Right now, she is stable, but she is in an unresponsive state. The cause has not been determined yet, but we are running tests. We will let you all know the status of her health as we move along."

Kenley spoke up very clearly with that assertive tone that usually gets people to move. "When can we go back and see our mother?"

"Right now, we are still doing some tests. It won't be long. I will see to it that you get back as quickly as possible." The doctor gave a quick smile then excused himself to go back to his patients.

The girls and I went to the waiting room. The TV had the *Price is Right* playing, and the contestants were at the final showcase. That meant that it was almost noon, and I still had not let Cynthia know what was going on or that I was in Savannah. I hoped that she would understand that I needed to be there for Ava Lynn and my girls, but if not she would just have to get over it. I really did not feel like talking, so I decided that I would do what the young folks do and send her a text. I typed, *Hey Cynthia, I had to come to Savannah. Ava Lynn is in the hospital, and I am here with the girls. Will call later with details.* I hit send. There. I fulfilled my obligation to communicate.

So, we sat and waited to see Ava Lynn. The waiting room had no windows, just those beige hospital walls and the not so comfortable chairs lined up right next to one another. The TV prompted us on how long we had been waiting as the programming changed from daytime soap operas to judge shows to the evening news, then to Cynthia's favorite game shows, Wheel of Fortune and Jeopardy.

The girls went to get food from nearby restaurants since the hospital food was not very good. Barnes, which was a seafood and barbeque restaurant, was close to the hospital. Kim-Kim announced there was no need to starve while we waited. She went to get us food and brought it back to the waiting room. We were the only family in there at that time, so we did not have to worry about the smell of the hickory-smoked meat tantalizing anyone. There were a few of the workers that poked their heads in asking why hadn't we brought enough for everyone. My girls just laughed off the comments, while I just stared at nothing really.

We had gotten about two or three updates throughout the day that were not very comforting to any of us since they still didn't know what went wrong. The report we got at about the time the gavel fell on one of the afternoon court shows was that she was placed on a ventilator because she needed help breathing. We knew that she was in the ICU, and most importantly, she was still alive.

Around the time that John Gilbert was telling us that "This…Is…. JEOPARDY," a new face entered the waiting room to let us know that we could go back one at a time to see Ava Lynn. The girls quickly retorted that they needed to go in together, but this nurse wasn't having it. She said what she meant, and she meant what she said, so we filed back one at a time to the ICU. They only allowed you to stay in there for a few minutes at a time. Visiting hours for the ICU were almost over, but we all were able to go in and let her know that we were there.

Each of the girls went back, and they spent every moment that the nurse said that they had left with their mom. I was the last one to go back, and I hesitated because I was not sure what I thought I was going to see. Other than the tube in her mouth, she just looked like she was resting.

I started our conversation just as I normally do. I talked to her and told her how my week had been going. I touched her right hand, and it was just as soft as it was when we first touched back in high school. I loved this woman so much. I guess some of that churchiness from Cynthia had rubbed off on me a little because I found myself in a full-blown prayer holding Ava Lynn's hand and asking that she be healed in Jesus' name. That prayer flowed out, and the power in it shocked me. *Did I just speak over my woman like that?* Well, when it is genuine, prayer is a supernatural and powerful thing. Just as I said amen, I felt a faint squeeze of my hand. I looked down at Ava Lynn. Her face was still in the same position with her eyes closed shut, and the monitors had not changed any of the beeping patterns. I knew that was her way of giving me a sign that she was going to pull through this thing and be just fine.

I got that sign, but it would be four more days of unresponsiveness before Ava Lynn would open her eyes. Once she did, it was as if someone flipped a switch and she was back to her old self. She was up fussing and ready to go home. The doctors never found out what made her slip away from us or slip back to us. Whatever it was will remain a mystery. What we do know is that she vowed never to get another colposcopy again.

I took Ava Lynn home, and this time, it felt like it was where I needed to be. It felt like this was where my home should be. I did not make any big announcements to anyone. I just made this my permanent residence. After the second week of me being in Savannah, Cynthia finally broke down and asked me, "When do you think you might make your way back home?"

"I'm not sure," poured from my mouth before I could think of something better to say. Cynthia and I had been married for over forty years, so she was used to me by now, and sometimes I felt like she knew me better than I knew myself. She gave me a simple reply, one that I definitely did not expect.

She said, "I will be in Savannah in about three hours. Meet me at the mall." Her words and her tone were very precise and exacting. She certainly was not requesting, but more so demanding that I be a specific place.

"Okay, just call me when you are about thirty minutes away."

"Alright, see you soon." Then a dial tone.

I was left to wonder what she could possibly want to meet me about and in Savannah of all places.

We decided over text to change our meeting location to the Shell House restaurant on I-95 and 204. *Was this a ploy for me to take her on a date?* Well, she was my wife after all so we would have dinner in the very least.

We ate, and everything between us flowed as normal. I paid the bill, and we continued our conversation as we walked out together. I grew weary and wanted to find the underlying cause of our forced date night.

"Cynt, did you have something that you wanted to talk about? Why did you drive all the way up to Savannah to meet me?" I asked. I didn't want to seem irritated because I truly wasn't. I was just curious about the motives behind it all.

When we reached her car, it became apparent to me what was going on. I saw boxes and suitcases piled up in the back seat. Cynthia unloaded everything onto the pavement, and for a woman who was over sixty, she slung everything out so fast, I did not even have time to argue.

"Kendall, I love you, but I am done with this. I cannot win in this fight against her, and I am too good of a person to have to beg my husband to come home. It is evident that you are where you really want to be. Since you asked, the reason that I asked you to meet me is so that I could give you your things."

She was right. This was where I wanted to be. Even though she was right in everything that she was saying, it still stung.

When I spoke, it was something that was probably not the best thing to say. However, it was what came to my mind. I said, "I guess you think this makes you free to go fuck around with Chuck again now, huh?" As soon as I said it, I wished that I could have taken it back.

"No, that is not what I will be doing, but I certainly will not be doing this with you any longer. I love you, Kendall Sanford. With all of my heart, I do, but I am too old and tired to have to keep putting up with this nonsense. You have true love, and I get it. Yes, I finally get that, and that true love is not me. I am your wife in name only, and I will not keep fighting for a man that don't want to be kept."

Emotionless is the only way to describe her. You could tell that she had thought long and hard about this decision. When a woman is finally done, there are no tears, no theatrics. What I just saw was my wife telling me that she was done with US. I watched her pull away as I loaded my belongings in my truck, then drove back home to Ava Lynn's house.

I did not feel like talking to Ava Lynn about the episode that I had with Cynthia, but I needed to talk to someone. I called my go-to, David. The phone rang three times, then the answering machine came on. I did not bother to leave a message. I just hung the phone up. It was not late, so I knew he was up watching one of his TV shows. My cellphone started to vibrate and ring not even a minute later.

"Hey, Kenny Boy! Sorry I missed you when you first called. I was trying to get to the phone, but the answering machine got to you first. What's going on?" I could tell that David was running or trotting because he sounded like he was out of breath.

"Hey, no worries. I was just calling because I needed to talk some stuff out. You know I am always in some shit." I wasn't lying. It was always something going on.

He did not waste any time. "Well let's hear it then, so I can get back to my shows."

I did not beat around the bush. I just blurted it out. "I think Cynthia just left my ass."

With confusion in his voice, he said, "What do you mean 'think'? Did she or didn't she leave you?"

"It was strange. We went to dinner, and everything was normal. Then when I got outside, she had suitcases and boxes with my shit in it all piled up in her car. Then she told me she loved me and left me standing there."

"Well, it's about time my sister-in-law got some sense about herself. She should have left you a long time ago."

I was shocked, but not really, by what he said to me. "I'm your brother. How can you say that? I have taken care of her, and she has never had to want for nothing all these years."

"See that's the problem right there. You can't even see when you are doing something that's wrong. I know you are not this blind to your own infidelity. Come on, man. You can't possibly be serious." He started chuckling after he said that last statement.

"Yeah, I'm serious. Cynthia shouldn't have any complaints, and I took care of my responsibilities. I have always been honest. She never guessed about where I was or about what I was doing."

"So, you think that makes that shit right? Let me answer that for you, HELL NO! You ain't right, and I don't know why she put up with you for all these years. She endured your many children by other women, and you shacked up with another woman for the entirety of your marriage. First Donna then Ava Lynn. How do you think that made her feel? Don't answer. I can tell you that, too. Like she wasn't good enough. When the truth is, she is a good woman, who I have watched over the years bow down to your every flight of fancy with other women. I'm just glad for her that she finally got up the nerve do it."

He was right even though I did not want to admit it. I wanted to be with Ava Lynn but did not want to leave Cynthia. Well, Cynthia made it clear where she stood on that, so I did not have to stress myself about it anymore. In the short time that it took to have dinner and get kicked to the curb, my life had been turned upside down. I headed out to the Thunderbolt pier because fishing always cleared my head when things just were not going right in my world. I stayed out there past dark, and I decided to get myself back to Ava Lynn's house before I wouldn't have anywhere at all to go.

Just as I was loading up my fishing gear in my truck, I felt a cold circle press up against my right temple, followed by a husky voice saying, "Don't move old man. You know what it is." Under the cover of night, this thug had crept up on me, and now the rest of my life was in his hands. Was this how it was going to end for me? I certainly hoped not, but the next few moments would be critical. Another husky demand came from behind me, "Give me your wallet and your car keys. You bet not thank about being a hero neither, old man."

"My wallet is in my glove box," I said without as much as a quiver in my voice. I was scared, but more pissed at myself for not seeing this kid slip up on me.

"Move your ass and get it then. Hurry up! Give me your watch and cell phone too while ya at it." He rushed me with his request. He was fidgeting the whole time. I was just hoping that his nervousness did not slip on the trigger of the pistol that was still to my temple.

"Alright, easy. I will give you everything you asked for," I coached as I started removing my watch. My watch, a Rolex, was a gift the twins had given me a few years back. I loved that watch, but I could replace it if necessary. "Here you go. What else did you need me to give you?" I questioned him.

"Oh, you being funny? Give me your motherfucking wallet! You stalling me, old man?" I could smell the fear in him. He was sweating so much he reminded of an animal in distress. I should have been the one that was sweating, but I moved calmly.

"Okay, I will get it right now. Son, you don't have to do this. There are more productive things that you could be doing. I could help you if let me." I tried to reason with the thug. I felt like if he thought he wouldn't get into trouble behind this, he would leave me be.

"You must want to die tonight. Keep fucking with me, and you're gonna have a new address over in Bonaventure Cemetery."

The hostility in his voice grew more intense as he said each word. I abandoned the notion that I might be able to reach this person and help him get on the right path in life. I went to get my wallet, and then I heard the "POPS."

Chapter 18

The officers talked to me as I sat in the ambulance being checked out by the paramedics. They checked my eyes, blood pressure, and every other vital sign that they possibly could. Officer Standifer, one of the people I knew from around town, was one of the folks on duty working the scene. He came over and patted me on the back.

"Kendall Sanford, I am sure glad you are okay. This could have ended so differently. Good thing you were quick on your feet," he said. I was not so sure how good I felt. As I looked at the white sheet covering the crumpled body that lied on the ground several feet away from me, I knew it was either him or me. However, I hated the fact that I even had to make that choice.

I looked over at Officer Standifer, and asked if he knew who the stick-up kid was? He told me he was a local twenty-two year old, who had his fair share of run-ins with the law. It was just a matter of time before he picked the wrong someone, and that was that night.

Just as soon as they cleared me, I called my attorney to let him know what had happened. We needed to keep my name, and the company's name, as far away from any bad PR as possible. All I could think about was these new aged families that try to sue the person for wrongful death when their relative tried to rob someone and ended up being killed in the process. In what universe does that even make sense? This one apparently.

The officers continued to collect evidence and got all my information. They said that they would call me in if they needed to ask any more questions. I found out later that one of the nearby homeowner's security camera caught the entire thing on film, so the police were able to corroborate my story and timeline.

I was free to drive home, and I went straight to Ava Lynn's. I pulled in the garage, and her car was in its usual spot. I opened the door to the house and was hit by the smell of something Italian cooking in the kitchen. I was not very hungry because my mind was on everything that had happened from Cynthia to the botched robbery. However, walking into that heavenly smell made my stomach change its mind, and I was ready to dive into whatever was cooking.

When Ava Lynn saw me, she immediately knew that something was not right. "Hey, Kendall, how was everything? You saw Cynthia, right? Was everything okay?"

"Yes, I did see Cynthia. Afterward, I went fishing at the pier. Some stickup kid tried to rob me." I figured if I made light of the situation, she might not get so excited. That tactic did not work.

"WHAT!?! Oh my Lord, Kendall! What happened? I knew something was wrong with you. Your clothes are all out of sorts. Did he hurt you? Tell me what happened." She was in such a frenzy I spent the next few minutes trying to assure her that I was all right and unharmed.

"Ava Lynn, what are you cooking? It sure does smell good." She told me that she had cooked rigatoni with vodka sauce, salad, garlic toast, and baked a lava cake for dessert. All of that sounded good, but first I needed to take a shower and get the day off of me. That robber smelled bad, but I think I smelled just as bad at that point.

After I took a shower, I put on a sweatsuit so that I could get comfortable. I ate dinner in front of the TV, which drove Ava Lynn crazy. I was not up to talking about what had happened with Cynthia at the restaurant or the robbery. I fell asleep in the recliner after I had eaten every piece of food she put on my plate. I must have been worn out from all that happened that day because I fell into a deep sleep like when the doctors put you to sleep for surgery.

The next morning, I was awakened by the smell of hot breakfast cooking on the stove. I gathered myself and looked over at the clock; it was almost nine-thirty. I knew company had to be coming over that day. She usually cooked pancakes when some of the grandkids were at the house. Everyone loved Ava Lynn's pancakes, including me, so that was always a great way to wake up.

When I went into the kitchen, pancakes, eggs, bacon, and a large glass of milk waited for me on the table. Ava was standing over the stove in her pink nightgown and fuzzy house slippers. Even as she aged, she still had a curvy figure that I loved to admire without her knowing. This woman still got my attention the same way that she did when we first met in high school. She must have felt me staring because she turned around and said, "Well, good morning, sleepyhead."

I walked over to her, gave her a pat on her behind and a kiss on the cheek. "Mornin', babe. Are we having company this morning or is all of this for me?"

She smiled only the way that she can and said, "I thought I would make an extra special breakfast for you since you had such a rough night last night." She paused for a minute, then continued. "You know I saw on the news this morning that there was a botched robbery over at that pier last night. Was that about you?"

"Well, I guess it was about me. Not real sure what you saw," I told her in no uncertain terms.

"Kendall, you know I am not going to do this with you. I gave you your space and didn't pressure you about talking about yesterday, but I need to know from you what happened." Her tone was very direct, and I knew that she meant business. I could've tried to put her off, but for my own sake, I figured I had better go full disclosure. I shared every single detail of my previous evening, starting with Cynthia all the way to the moment I walked in the door at her house. She was in full-blown tears once I got to the very end.

"See this is why I didn't want to tell you last night. I didn't want to relive that scene all over again," I told her.

"I am sorry that you had to go through all of that yesterday. I didn't see you come in with any bags. Where is your stuff that Cynthia gave you?"

Until then, I had forgotten about it. "Out in the garage. I'll go get everything later."

"I am sure you will have a busy day today with all that was going on. Do you know what next steps you have to take? Have you already contacted the attorney?"

"Honestly, I plan to just take it step by step. I am not thinking about a full plan. I still have a great deal to process, babe. I killed another human being last night. I almost died myself. It came down to him or me, and babe, I cannot believe it. I carry my piece for peace of mind, and I actually had to use it on someone. I may be going in for questioning, testifying and Lord knows what else at this point. I don't know what to expect, but all I know for sure is that I can only take all of this one day at a time. Even with Cynthia, one day at a time. The man with all the answers has no answers today. I am not going to sweat it, though. There is nothing I can do about the past, so I will just look to move forward, and let everything fall where it may."

All of that information sunk in on Ava while we ate our breakfast in mostly silence. We both tried to make light conversation, but all the air was taken out of the room after my revelation. I am glad that she did not press the issue anymore. Women usually like to talk about feelings. *How does this make you feel? Are you okay with this? Well, now that I know can we talk about it a little more?* When I am grilled with one of those, I want to respond like "HOW ABOUT HELL NO! SHUT UP ALREADY WITH THE QUESTIONS!" I am not crazy though so I would never actually say that aloud, only in my head.

The morning went by slowly, but when I received a call from my attorney, the pace of the day began to pick up. He told me to come over to his office so that he could give me insight on the next steps that I would need to take as we got past all this "botched robbery" business. After talking with him, I felt more at ease about everything. I was even briefed on what to do if the family of the robber tried to make a civil suit against me. That would come down to whose pockets ran deeper, and from what I could tell, I thought I would come out on top in that situation, too. But, I could have been wrong. Truthfully, I was just praying it wouldn't even get that far.

As soon as I started wrapping everything up with the attorney, my phone started to blow up with calls from the children. I just let them go to voicemail. I would deal with them later. There was no need in rehashing the story that many times. I started feeling less anxious and more grateful that I wasn't the one with the white sheet over me.

I sent a text to all of the kids that lived in Savannah or nearby and asked them to come by the house at 6:30 for dinner. If they could not make it, I would understand, but I suddenly wanted my children and grandchildren around me. I told them that I would talk to all of them at the same time tonight. Everyone responded that they would be there. I called Ava Lynn and told her that I invited everyone over for dinner. She did not put up a fuss at all. She said okay and asked me what I felt like having. This is why I loved Ava so much. She understood me. Always had and always would. I also called Kevin and Janie Mae to invite their families over for dinner, too. It was a rare occasion to stare death in the face and live to walk away from it.

***

Crabs were cracking, and the laughter was overflowing, as all of the family had made it in. Ava Lynn ordered a low country boil from the local seafood store. You could always tell the good ones because there would be a case with iced down fish on display as soon as you walked in the door, handwritten signs hanging all over the place, and a huge sign to tell you that you couldn't get cooked food with your peach card or food stamp card. Those places always seemed to be run by Asians and were always located in predominantly Black neighborhoods. No one ever questioned why there were no black-owned seafood shops or even convenience stores for that matter. It was just the status quo for our city.

I had given the run-down of the events for the past two days, leaving out the part that Cynthia had kicked me out. Everyone was happy that I was still alive and in one piece, and all pledged to be supportive of everything that would happen in the next few months. It felt great to have my family around me. Even though everyone couldn't be there, it was great to see those that could make it. The twins stayed close by me all night, and even Janie Mae got in a few extra hugs. It was good to love and be loved.

"Janie Mae, come show me that new line dance that you were trying to tell me about that you learned in your class," Ava Lynn said.

"Oh, it's the Michael Jackson," she replied. "Kim-Kim, can you pull up that song *They Don't Care* by Michael Jackson and play it on the speaker."

Kim-Kim played the song, and all of us joined in to learn the steps to the line dance. One thing I can say about us is we all loved to dance. The only thing we did not do this particular night was get knee-deep into a game of spades. The laughter and being together was enough. It was evident that the most important thing was that I was safe, and we could all celebrate another day on this side together.

Once the music died down, I headed to the bedroom to take a bathroom break when I heard my cell phone ringing. I looked at the caller ID, and it was Cynthia. I figured she must have heard what had happened and now wanted to play the sorry game.

"Hello." I answered before it went to voicemail.

"Hey, Kendall. It's me, Cynthia. I heard what happened, and I just wanted to call and hear your voice. Are you alright?"

"Yeah, I am alright. I am just going to take things one day at a time until we get past all of this."

"All I wanted was to make sure that you were okay," Cynthia told me. I could tell that she wanted to say more but was purposefully keeping her conversation short.

"Thank you for calling to check on me, Cynthia. I want you to know that despite what you may feel towards me or about my choices, I do love you. It means a great deal to me that you took the time to reach out to me after you told me that you were done. You are my wife, and no matter what, I will always be here for you, just like I know that if I need anything, you will be there for me, too."

With a slight whimper in her voice, she said, "I love you, Kendall. I'm glad you are okay. Goodbye." Then just like that, she was gone. I could not dwell on that conversation then. I needed to get back to my guests.

Just then, Ava sauntered into the bedroom and hugged me tight around my neck. "I think you were able to answer everyone's questions tonight, and I know the girls were happy to see for themselves that you are doing alright." Then she kissed me perfectly like only she could, and that made me feel like so much was lifted off me.

Chapter 19

My brother, David, began a tradition where the men in the family would take a guy's only trip once a year. With every passing year, the trips would get larger and better. It was a time to bond with all of the brothers, sons, sons-in-law, nephews, and grandsons of the family.

That same year we were off to Arizona to golf at one of the many resorts that they had out that way. A friend of David's owns the one that we would be staying in, so we got the royal treatment. I was never a huge fan of the game of golf. I think Tiger Woods sparked the interest for many black folks to start playing, but I personally just went to drink beer and enjoy time with the fellas. I did not have to hit a golf ball at all. I would be perfectly content driving the golf cart all day, but David would never allow that to happen. We all had to play. If our bodies were able, he harassed us all into being willing participants.

The majority of us were able to make the trip that year with the exception of Karissa's husband, Jameson. He had to study for the bar exam. I was not going to protest because he needed to pass in order to take care of my baby girl appropriately. I never really cared for him much, but Karissa Joy loved him, so there was not much I could do about that.

After a long day on the links, we showered before heading to dinner and retreating to Cohiba cigars on the deck at the villa. All three of my sons were on the trip, and I enjoyed having them all together. My goal with Kendall Junior and Kenneth was to make sure that even though they had different mothers, they were close. Since I did not know about Lamont until much later, I just wanted him to know that he was a Sanford, even if his mom gave him a different last name.

As we sat out in the cool of the desert night with cigar smoke looming overhead like a smokestack at the paper mill, we all felt a sense of peace with the world.

Of all of my children, Lamont seemed to always be the one with the most straightforward questions about my life. Tonight would be no different. "Pops, how is it that you remained married for so long? You and Ma Cynt been married for over fifty years, and I know that I came along during that time from my mom. How are y'all able to make it work?"

I could tell this was a genuine question, and though it was a good question, I was unsure of the best way to answer.

"I know what people often said about me. They would liken my lifestyle to that old Temptation's song, *Papa Was a Rolling Stone*. Well, during one point in my life that was true except my vice was cocaine, not drinking." I took a long draw on my cigar and blew smoke up in the air and continued. "That was before you were born, or before I knew about you being my son. Me and Cynthia always had an understanding. I always wanted my boys to be better than me, so I won't lie to you. Me and Cynthia got married under the guidance of her preacher daddy, and his gun when he found out she was pregnant from me. I promised her in that church 'til death do us part,' and that meant something to me. It was just that I was one of those lucky souls to find multiple women that over the years have played a special part in my life. Take your mama, for instance. Yes, we met during a turbulent time in my life, but she made sure that I was taken care of during that time. You see, Cynthia put me out because she wasn't going to put up with my drug use and abusive behavior. Your mama loved me enough through the bad part. She didn't tell me about you because she felt ashamed that she made a baby with a married man. Your mother was a good woman to me and was a special part of my story. Just like Donna and Ava Lynn are both significant pieces to the puzzle that is me. Through everything, I remained honest with Cynthia about what I was doing and my intentions. Most men get caught up because they try to sneak and do dirt behind their lady's back. That was not how I operated. You could either take me as I am, or you leave. Whichever one you choose, I am still going to be Kendall Sanford at the end of the day. So, to answer your question, we remained together for so long due to honesty and me never trying to hide things from her. I had a home with all my ladies at one point or another, but I still had my wife at the end of the day. I know that you all have had your thoughts about your father over the years. Before I leave this earth, I want each of you to know that I loved each of your mothers in their own special way. My brothers always teased me that I was going to get shot one day keeping all the women that I did, but in reality, it wasn't a lot of women. It was just the same women over a long period of time. "

Kevin chimed in here. "Yeah, I told you many times that I don't see how you were able to pull that off. Lou would have cut off precious body parts if I even so much as thought about having separate households. It has worked for you, and I can say that over the years you have never let any of your responsibilities slide. Once you found out about Lamont, you brought him into the family circle without hesitation. You may have gone about it in an odd way, but you have always been a true man and taken care of your family business."

"Wow, Kevin! From you, that means a lot. You always painted me to be this big-time gigolo. Thank you, man." I tried not to get choked up because being the youngest, I was always given a hard time by my brothers about my choices. It really meant a lot to me.

Lamont responded, "I get it. You were a rolling stone just not in the same sentiment as the song exactly. Where you laid your hat, you spread love, and you loved us hard. You made sure we never wanted for anything, and you showed us what a real example of a man was."

I did not respond. I just listened and took in what he was saying. I hope this helped him in some way. This was definitely something that I knew had been on his mind. I could tell in the way he asked the question. I hoped this also helped everyone else in the family to somewhat understand the dynamics of my relationships. I never needed or wanted any of their approval, but it did feel good to know that they somehow understand me a little better now. It was a strange feeling that I got, but I liked hearing my son say that I was a true example of how to be a man for him. In all that I did wrong in my life, I guess I did do something right.

Chapter 20

After four months of giving Cynthia her space, I decided that enough time had passed. I went to Darien to our house. I wanted to get some more of my things and talk to Cynthia. I called her ahead of time to let her know that I would be coming because I did not want to have another case of murder on my hands. If I saw another man in my house, I am not quite sure how that would play out for me. Plus, I was too old to think about that so to avoid any confusion, I gave her fair warning so that nobody else would be sitting up in my house.

When I went to the door, I had a thought. *What if she changed the locks?* I slid the key in, and the door opened for me. Crisis avoided. Everything still looked the same as when I left. I am not sure what I expected, but it sure did feel good being in my familiar surroundings.

Cynthia's car was in the garage, but I did not see her. The house was quiet.

"Cynthia, are you home?" I bellowed out. The silence was the only response I received. I walked in the bedroom to see if Cynthia might be in the shower, but there was still no sign of her. Then the house phone rang. When I picked it up, the hesitation in the caller's greeting let me know she was shocked to hear my voice on the other end of the phone.

"Daddy, is that you? What are you doing at home?" It was Karissa. She was calling to check in on her mother. She talked to her every day if not every few hours.

"Hey, baby girl. Yes, I'm here. Can't a man come to his own house when he wants to?"

"Sure, you can. How are you doing today? When am I going to see you, anyway? Jameson passed his exam! I am planning a party for him. When I get everything organized, I will send out invites. I hope that you will be able to come." She sounded so happy.

"I sure do miss you, baby girl. If it fits into my schedule, you can count on me being there. You know we are due for a father-daughter lunch soon. Let me know when you're free, so I can take you out to your favorite place."

"That sounds great, Daddy. We certainly can get that on the schedule. I have to travel for work, but once I get back, we are making a date." I could envision her smile as she spoke.

"Great! Now for why you were really calling. I just got here, and I don't know where your mother is. Her car is in the garage, but I don't see any signs of her in the house. When I see her, I will tell her to call you back," I told her.

Karissa replied, "No worries, Daddy. I will try to reach her on her cell phone."

We said our goodbyes and hung up the phone. A few moments later, I heard Cynthia's cell phone ringing from the nightstand. I looked, and it was Karissa.

I answered Cynthia's phone. "Hey, sweetie. Her cell phone is here in the room. She must have gone out for a walk or something. She will call you back soon."

As I looked around the room, I saw her purse on the closet door and her keys on the dresser in their normal spot. *Where on earth was Cynthia?* Maybe it was best that we had not run into each other. I thought about some of the stuff that I had out in the shed in the backyard. I could not remember if there was anything I wanted, so I thought that I would go out there and look. When I left out of the sliding doors that lead to the backyard, I had not noticed too much different. The azaleas and hydrangeas looked pretty and gave a blue and white color scheme to the backyard. Then I saw something move in the corner of my right eye and heard a sound that South Georgia folks could recognize anywhere. There was a rattler in the yard, and this was one of those snakes that you did not ever want to find slithering around.

In all of my years, I had never seen one this close to the house. We would usually see them out in the woods when we were running pulpwood or out hunting. I saw the shovel over near the shed where I was heading. I did not make any quick moves because I didn't want the snake to strike at me. Once I had the shovel, it was good-bye for Mr. Snake. One good chop to the head and he was no longer a problem. When I was a kid, anytime my mama saw a snake anywhere near our yard, this was how she dealt with it. She would always say, "The best kind of snake is a dead snake." I was just glad that I saw it instead of Cynthia. She would have put on a show like no other. I don't think I had ever met another person who grew up in the country and was so afraid of every kind of critter.

After killing the rattler and digging in the shed, I worked up an appetite. I went back into the house and found some food in the refrigerator. Cynthia always made sure there was food in the house, no matter how many people were there. I saw some leftover pepper steak and gravy. I put that over some rice and had a great microwaved meal. As I was finishing up, I heard the back door open, and the sound of Cynthia laughing. The other voice was coming from our neighbor, Claudia. Claudia was one of the loudest people I had ever met, and she had a distinct accent. It sounded like a mix of Jamaican with this Geechee that we talk. I don't know why she had such an accent. She grew up out here in the same woods that we did. She would always tell the story that her daddy was some creole from Louisiana, and she would go spend the summers with him. She said that he was a great big light-skinned man who almost looked white if you did not know better. That was where she said she got her fair skin from because her mama was as black as the tar on the road. Wherever she got that accent from, I knew I was not in any mood to deal with her loudness today.

"Oh, looky what the cat drug in," Claudia said as she spotted me sitting at the table finishing my lunch.

"Hey, Claudia. Good to see you." I mustered up a smile, hoping that she would be on her way.

"Good to see you, too, neighbor. Me and your wife here just went and got us some exercise at that new senior center that they put up in town. It is so nice! You gotta go see it if you haven't already been." The way Claudia drug out the word nice grated my nerves, but I tried to be as polite as I could. Her presence was simply annoying me. I greeted Cynthia, then excused myself to the back room. I did not come back out until I heard her leave a few minutes later.

"I see your neighbor is still as loud as she always was," I said.

"I forgot how much she aggravates you. You know you could try to disguise it a little better when she is around. She really is a great person."

"But does she have to always be so loud?" I asked. Having known her for over twenty years and nothing changed in that time, I already knew the answer to that question.

"She is who she is, just like you are who you are."

I felt like that was some sort of jab at me, but I was unsure of how to take it. "So how exactly am I?"

"Kendall Sanford, you are old and set in your ways. That is how you are," she quickly told me. "You like everything how you like it, and nothing can veer you from that path. It's Kendall's way or the highway."

Cynthia did not skip a beat with what she was doing or even notice that I was looking for her to continue her explanation. Oh well. I knew better than to push the envelope. There was no need to get into a fight about it. She had already spoken her piece about me, and I was only there to get a few items and head back to my life in Savannah.

"Cynthia, how have you been doing? It has been a long time since we actually talked. Anything new happening?" I asked in an attempt to get a meaningful conversation going.

Standing there at five foot nothing, she smiled at me with a warmth that I did not think I would ever see again. "I am doing real good, Kendall. I have had such peace in my life these past few months. Maybe I should have kicked you out long ago so I could feel as good as I have been feeling lately," she told me with a little laugh.

"Glad to know that I was able to bring that smile back to your face, even if it was due to me leaving."

"Kendall, I won't lie. I miss you something awful, but I can't continue to live how we have been living. It does not make me happy. When I said a few minutes ago it's either your way or the highway, this is what I was talking about. I told you that I did not want you to be with her anymore, and the one thing that I asked of you, you refuse to do. So, it became crystal clear to me. You do not care about my feelings as your wife. Therefore, I can no longer care about or have you as my husband. I have been able to spend time in prayer and meditation about what is the right thing for me to do. Kendall, I am ready to get a divorce, and you are free and clear to marry the 'love of your life.' That is what you call her, right?" Cynthia ended with a rhetorical question that I dared not answer.

"Cynthia, I love you and the family that we have raised. We are in our golden years. Why would we part ways now? Do you just need more alone time before I can come back home?"

"Kendall, the Bible tells us that 'My people will abide in a peaceful habitation, in secure dwellings.' Every time I think about you in Savannah with Ava Lynn, my house is not peaceful, and my dwellings are not secure. As old as we are, I still have to put up with this bullshit. No woman in her right mind would have dealt with this. First, it was Donna, then it was Ava Lynn. All while you were supposed to be MY husband."

"Cynthia, so what do you think I am going to do? Just let you end this marriage just like that?" I questioned her while shrugging my shoulders.

"Let me get this straight, and you need to hear me clearly. You ain't gon' LET me do nothing. I have a mind, and I know how to use it." She motioned her hand, signaling she and I, and said, "See this right here? This is over."

When she said that all I remember is a sharp pain hitting me in my chest like a bolt of lightning, and I blacked out.

Chapter 21

I opened my eyes, and all I saw was light, light, light, and more light. I couldn't really move around, but I heard a faint sound that reminded me of Karissa Joy. *Where am I, and what is going on?* I closed my eyes and opened them again. I felt a kiss on my cheek, followed by a voice saying, "I love you, Daddy."

"I love you, too, baby girl," I replied.

Then I saw Cynthia in front of me. "Cynthia, where am I? What is happening?" I think that is what I tried to ask her, but the words were muffled as if something was in my mouth.

I could see people rushing to where I was, and hear more noises as machines started going off. I felt my arm get warm, and then I went back to sleep.

The next time I woke up, there was darkness with very little light. I tried to move my arms and my feet, but nothing would work. When I looked up this time, there were little flecks of crystals in the white ceiling. This ceiling was familiar to me. It was the ceiling at home. Then I heard an unfamiliar voice say my name a few times. I did not respond because I was not sure of who it was. Then I felt someone grab my hand. I heard the voice say, "If you understand me, wiggle your fingers." I wiggled them then I heard voices that were a little more familiar. A woman who I never had seen before appeared in front of me, leaning in from my right. Next, I saw Cynthia lean in from my left. I was tired, so I closed my eyes again.

This time I had a dream that took me back to some of the best and most important times in my life. The majority of my memories were filled with all of my family members. Cynthia was front and center in most of my dream. In my reflections, I realized how much she had played a part in my happiness. She never wavered in her love for me and stuck by my side all of these years. Being with me had been no picnic for damn sure, and all she wanted was my undivided attention and affection. I felt like I was taking care of her because she never worked, but all of her needs weren't met. I did not understand that I had been emotionally unavailable because I refused to see what she was asking of me. Maybe I was selfish. I wanted it all, and I could not see how much pain my actions really caused her deep down inside. No wonder she fell into another man's arms. I allowed that to happen by not paying her any attention. As the thoughts swirled in my head, I felt like opening my eyes to escape my mind. This time when I opened my eyes, there was Cynthia right in front of me looking as beautiful as ever.

"Cynthia, I need to tell you something," I tried to say. It came out muffled, but I think she understood me.

"Oh, Kendall, you need to rest now. I don't want you trying to talk and strain yourself. Just rest now," she told me.

I was tired, but I had to say what was on my mind. "Cynthia, I gotta say this. I am not sure that I will get another chance." I took a pull on the oxygen that was running under my nose and said, "I want you to know that I do love you, and I appreciate you as my wife." As I was talking, I could see the water start to collect in the corners of her eyes. "I know that over the years, I have hurt you, and I regret that I wasn't always the best for you. Please know that I did the best I could do by you. There is nothing that I can do about it now but tell you this. When I leave this place, I want you to be as happy as possible." I closed my eyes for a prolonged blink. When I opened my eyes again, Cynthia was still right there attentive and hanging on to the moment. "Cynthia, please tell all the kids that I love them, and I know that each of them will be alright. Tell them not to cry for me because I did my job here on earth, which was to raise them. Cynt, I think we did a mighty fine job raising the kids, don't you agree?"

She smiled and shook her head. The water fell down her cheeks in waves. She held my hand gently, and the warmth generated made me feel like all was well.

"Cynthia, one last request before I go back to sleep." I took another pull on the oxygen, and said, "Thank you for being the best wife to a man that did not deserve you." Looking deep into her eyes, I told her, "Girl, you shole is cute! Give me a kiss."

Cynthia obliged, and I fell asleep again. Only this time, I never opened my eyes again.

Chapter 22

"Kendall Sanford was one of the hardest working men that any of us have ever known," Kim-Kim told the church. "He was my personal hero and the type of person that a girl was proud to call Daddy. My siblings and I want to thank each of you for coming out today to help us celebrate the life of our father. Though he may not be here with us in the physical realm, he lives on through his children and his grandchildren. Again, thank you and God bless each of you."

That's my girl! She held it together and spoke so eloquently about me. What a nice service Cynthia and the kids held for me. As much as Cynthia loved me, she knew that Ava Lynn loved me, too. I was glad that she was the woman that I knew she would be and included her in the services. I am sure that the program confused all of my friends in Savannah who thought that Ava Lynn and I were married. In true Cynthia style, she laid it all out there so no one would question anything. My obituary read:

He leaves to cherish his memory, his wife of sixty years, Cynthia Sanford; Dear friend and long-time companion Dr. Ava Lynn Stevens of Savannah GA; Children Kendall Jr. (Samantha) of Savannah, GA, Kenneth of Hampton, VA, Kimberly Middleton (Broderick) of Savannah, GA, Kenley Beckett (John), of Savannah, GA, Lamont Cundiff (Terinita) of Brunswick, GA, and Karissa Joy Mathews (Jameson); Brothers Lester (Lottie Bell) of Brunswick, Ga, Kevin (Louvinia) of Savannah, GA, and David (Patricia) of Charlotte, NC; Sister Janie Mae Stevens (Theophilus) of Savannah, GA; 12 grandchildren, 3 great-grandchildren, and a host of nieces, nephews, and other relatives and friends.

In hindsight, we all have things that we have done of which we are not proud of. There are situations that you will reflect on and think to yourself, *I could have handled that a little better.* Before I died, I was able to tell my wife how I felt about her. About the things that I wish I could have changed between us. On more than one occasion, she had cared for me and nursed me back to health. Most women would have left me out to rot, but not Cynthia. Even though she told me that I was causing her pain, I could not see it for my own selfish needs. Not everyone gets the chance to apologize to those that they have wronged. I am just glad that Cynthia was able to know I did hear her.

Made in the USA
Monee, IL
03 March 2020

22559440R00104